Evil

Martha stared at her. Something about the way Wynn was looking back at her made her uneasy. "What . . . about my house?"

"Hey, Wynn!" Blake yelled. The Jaguar was moving slowly towards them, and Blake was hanging out the window. "Hurry up! Greg's got a meeting!"

Wynn wasn't even listening to him; her expression was on Martha, and it looked suddenly strained. "You . . . really don't know, do you? Nobody told you—"

Martha shook her head. "Are you talking about the old cemetery?"

And Wynn was looking so strange—sort of sad and sympathetic at the same time, and Martha took a step back, not wanting to hear any more—

"There was a murder in your house," Wynn said quietly. "Everyone knows the old Bedford place is evil."

Also in the
Point Horror series:

April Fools
by Richie Tankersley Cusick

My Secret Admirer
by Carol Ellis

The Lifeguard
by Richie Tankersley Cusick

Beach Party
by R. L. Stine

Funhouse
by Diane Hoh

The Baby-sitter
by R. L. Stine

Teacher's Pet
by Richie Tankersley Cusick

Look out for:

The Boyfriend
by R. L. Stine

The Snowman
by R. L. Stine

The Invitation
by Diane Hoh

The Baby-sitter II
by R. L. Stine

The Girlfriend
by R. L. Stine

Mother's Helper
by A. Bates

Point Horror

TRICK OR TREAT

Richie Tankersley Cusick

Hippo Books
Scholastic Children's Books
London

Scholastic Children's Books,
Scholastic Publications Ltd,
7-9 Pratt Street, London NW1 0AE, UK

Scholastic Inc.,
730 Broadway, New York, NY 10003, USA

Scholastic Canada Ltd,
123 Newkirk Road, Richmond Hill,
Ontario, Canada L4C 3G5

Ashton Scholastic Pty Ltd,
P O Box 579, Gosford, New South Wales,
Australia

Ashton Scholastic Ltd,
Private Bag 1, Penrose, Auckland,
New Zealand

First published in the USA by Scholastic Inc., 1989
Published in the UK by Scholastic Publications, 1991

Text copyright © Richie Tankersley Cusick, 1989

ISBN 0 590 76421 7

10 9

Printed and bound in Great Britain by
Cox & Wyman Ltd, Reading

for Thea
who made me believe it could happen . . .
my love and gratitude

TRICK OR TREAT

Chapter 1

"Okay, how about this? 'Spirits in torment! Do they really come back to the scenes of their tragedies? Bound there forever, even in death?' "

Martha stared out at the deepening twilight, the rolling hillsides so unfamiliar, the trees nearly stripped by October winds. In spite of the station wagon's stuffy interior, she shivered.

"Dad, do we have to talk about that now?"

Mr. Stevenson gave a vague nod, his eyes focused more on his thoughts than on the road. "What a great topic for my new article! Guess Halloween's got me inspired and — " He stole a glance in her direction, his attention complete now. "Are you still upset with me?"

Martha let the words hang between them for several seconds. "I just . . . can't believe you did this."

Dad regarded her, his eyes shifting guiltily back to the windshield. "Now, you and I *talked* about this, Martha — you knew Sally and I wanted to get married and have all of us together. I couldn't have lived in the same house where Sally's ex used to live. And Sally and Conor could never have competed with all your mother's memories at home. It wouldn't have been fair for any of us. We had to get a place of our own."

"But you didn't have to elope — and you could have waited till Thanksgiving vacation to move — "

"Martha . . ." he said helplessly, "I just wanted to be with her."

"But *Sally* got the house. *She* picked it out and — "

"Hey, be reasonable. You and I agreed a long time ago to get out of the city. *I* didn't have time to go house-hunting, and when Sally called about this place, it sounded perfect. A study where I can write, a studio where Sally can paint — " He glanced at her again, his face tired. "You really . . . don't like her."

"No, Dad, it's not that. I like Sally. Honest."

"Conor, then."

"Conor's weird," she sighed. "Look, Dad — "

"You always wanted a big brother."

"He's *only* a year older than me."

"And think how much harder this'll be for him, being a senior and having to transfer in midyear — "

"Nothing bothers Conor," Martha said flatly.

"You've only met him a couple of times! He's a philosopher." Dad chuckled. "You just have to scratch below the surface and try to understand him."

"I don't want to understand him. I don't even want to be around him." How could anyone under-

stand a guy so aloof and casual about everything?
"He has that look," Martha said stubbornly.

"What look?"

"You know — like he can't make up his mind
whether to laugh at me or be disgusted." Dad was
making every effort not to laugh at her now, but
she knew she was right. Unreadable, that was
Conor. Independent and maddeningly elusive.

"He's always been nice to you, hasn't he?" Dad
asked.

"He just seems so . . . I don't know . . .
otherworldly."

"Otherworldly! Like an alien?"

"Oh, Dad, stop kidding — you know what I
mean! He hardly ever talks. When he does, it's more
like he's talking to himself. And he kind of leans
back and takes everything in — like he knows some
secret about life and he's just watching everyone
else make fools of themselves."

"Maybe he does," Dad smiled. "And maybe we
are."

"Oh, forget it — you just keep defending him."

"I think he fascinates you, and you won't admit
it."

"Dad, get serious — "

"Martha, you're just too — " Dad broke off
abruptly, the car slamming to a halt as he pointed
towards a shadowy break in the trees ahead. "This
is it, I think. Sally said the first clearing after that
turn back there."

Martha squinted through the dusk, shaking her
head. "I don't know . . . I can't see a thing." As the

car inched forward, branches clawed at her door. She heard the hollow clatter of a bridge under the wheels as they went deeper into the woods. "We're in the middle of nowhere! Maybe we should turn around and — "

"Look, Martha, there it is."

And Martha gripped the dashboard and stared.

The house looked strangely ghostlike, rising up through pale wisps of fog, its dark stone walls and chimneys interwoven with bare, twisted trees. Silhouetted there in the twilight, its gables crawled with dead ivy, its tattered awnings drooping like eyelids hiding secrets. Like something in a dream, not quite real. *Not quite safe. . . .*

Martha took a deep breath and let her eyes wander over the blur of house and shadows, the gloom broken here and there by sallow squares of window light. Someone had propped a scarecrow against the porch, and its hideous face flickered at her in the sputtering glow of a jack-o'-lantern. There was a long, low whine of autumn wind; as dead leaves spattered across the windshield, Martha glanced nervously towards the woods, her hands suddenly cold. *What a perfect place for someone to hide . . . for someone to watch . . . And we'd never even know. . . .*

"Perfect," Dad muttered, a grin spreading from ear to ear. "Absolutely perfect!" As he parked the car at the end of the drive, Sally came running out the front door, laughing and waving, catching them each in a hug.

"So what do you think?" Sally pulled Martha up

the wide steps onto the porch. "Pretty wonderful, huh?"

Martha gazed at the cracked door, the paint peeling off in long strips, the broken panes of stained glass carelessly taped over. Part of the boards had rotted away underfoot.

"Well," Sally said quickly, seeing Martha's look, "of course it still needs work! But what potential!"

"It's . . ." Martha nodded dumbly, "a wonderful house." *If you like horror movies.* "We'll love it here." *I wish I was on the other side of the world.* She glanced up and stiffened. For a moment she'd forgotten all about Conor, but as he stepped outside, the light from the hallway caught his face, and she felt herself irresistibly drawn to him like she'd been before.

There was just something about Conor. That weird something she couldn't quite pinpoint, and yet it was there, so real and just beyond figuring out, that it made her crazy. The square jaw and the way his mouth was always set — like he might be speculating over something — except the corners lifted slightly in a secret sort of amusement. The deep-set eyes — so cool and steady and piercingly blue beneath low brows. He was tall and slender, but his shoulders were broad, and tonight he was wearing jeans and a bulky sweater, those strong shoulders hunched against the chilly night air. His hair was thick and always looked windblown, burnished gold and tousled across his shoulders. Martha took him in with a sudden, sinking revelation.

My stepbrother. Oh, God, he's my stepbrother now.

She didn't have to like it. Not ever. She ducked past him into the house but not before catching that glint of amusement in the stare he gave right back to her. And then he and Dad were talking and shaking hands, and Sally was pulling on her again.

"You remember Conor, don't you? Gosh, listen to me — of *course* you remember Conor! Why am I so nervous, anyway — after all, we're family now!"

Martha stiffened again as Conor slipped one arm around her shoulders, giving her a hug. A slow, controlled smile inched across his lips, and she could feel herself turning red.

"My very own little sister. What a lucky guy."

Martha jerked out of his grasp as Dad and Sally choked back laughter.

"Uh, Conor, why don't you show Martha her room," Sally stammered. "Conor picked the one he thought you'd like, Martha, but of course if there's another — "

"I'm sure it'll be fine," Martha said tightly. Conor's glance slid over her, and he led the way upstairs.

It was too dark to really see much. As Martha followed the vague outline of Conor's back, she tried to pull away from the deep shadows, the close walls, the old musty smells. The stairs were warped and creaky, and as they came out onto the second floor, she stood there uncertainly, listening to Conor's hand groping along the wall.

"Half these lights don't work," he mumbled. "One

of the few minor inconveniences we'll have to get used to."

"What're the others?" Martha hated to ask.

There was a soft spurt of yellow light as several wall lamps came to life, illuminating part of a hallway. Conor squinted at them. "How does one bathroom strike you?"

Martha groaned. "You've got to be kidding. . . ."

"I wish I were. It's at the end of the servants' hall." At her puzzled expression, he nodded towards one black doorway. "There's a back staircase there, too — you can take it all the way to the cellar or up to the attic."

Martha peeked cautiously into a room. "Is this one mine?"

"No, it's back here — away from everyone else's."

Martha went slowly towards the last doorway, her uneasiness growing. There were so many shadows — shadows the lights couldn't touch — and Conor's voice sounded hollow and unnatural. She felt her heart flutter in her chest. "Why did you pick this room?"

"I thought you'd want privacy." He found the light and motioned her in. "Mom brought this bed down from the attic. You can use it till — what's wrong?"

Martha froze beside him on the threshold, her eyes riveted to the room beyond. There were shadows here, too — lots of them — skittering across the faded flowers on the torn, stained wallpaper. A bare window seat stretched beneath a curtainless window, and the closet door stood slightly ajar.

"It's so cold," she murmured.

Conor followed her gaze to the scant furnishings. "Once you get your own things, it won't seem so — "

"No." Martha looked up at him, her cheeks suddenly pale, and one hand grabbed for his sleeve. "Can't you feel it — it's so *cold* — it's so — "And as her grip tightened on his arm, the coldness turned to fear. "Conor . . . something terrible happened in this room."

For a long moment Conor stared at her, his face expressionless. She heard Sally calling them to dinner, and she saw the deep intensity of Conor's eyes, and she pulled away, suddenly mortified.

Conor was still watching her. "Drafts," he said quietly. "All old houses have them."

She nodded stiffly and followed him back downstairs.

She couldn't eat. Picking at the mysterious concoction on her plate, she was only vaguely aware of conversations going on around her, until she felt Conor nudging her under the table.

"Martha, you haven't heard a thing we've said," Dad scolded.

"Oh . . . sorry . . . I. . . ."

"Well, at least *someone* around here thinks my article is a stroke of genius — 'The Doomed and Restless Dead!' And I certainly have the inspiration for it," Dad chuckled. "Did the realtor guarantee ghosts with this place?"

"Could be," Sally grinned. "There's supposed to

be an old cemetery somewhere on the property."

Martha nearly choked. "A cemetery!"

"You shouldn't have told her," Conor shook his head. "She'll be packed up before dessert."

Sally glanced apologetically at Martha's bowed head. "I think you'll really like the school here, Martha. When you go on Monday, you're to see a Mr. — what's his name? — anyway, he'll be your advisor. Maybe you could kind of stick with Conor — he already knows his way around, and I know it'll seem strange to you the first few days."

Not any stranger than all of this, Martha thought, but aloud she said, "I'll be okay by myself."

Dad put down his fork. "Now look here, Martha. Sally's gone to an awful lot of trouble and I — "

"No trouble. Really. None," Sally insisted quickly, and Martha's food stuck fast in her throat. "I just thought Conor could show her where things are."

"I'd better stick close to her," Conor announced so matter-of-factly that everyone stared at him. "She looks about twelve. If I'm not there to vouch for her, they might send her over to the elementary school."

Martha gritted her teeth as Dad and Sally began laughing. It was true, she *had* always looked young for her age — wholesome, that's what Mom had always called her. Wide gray eyes and bouncy blonde hair, and a face that couldn't hide her true feelings, no matter how hard she tried. And she was trying now, but Conor was watching her, and she had that awful, exposed feeling that he could see right through her — and was enjoying himself.

"Thanks, Sally, good dinner," Martha lied. "May I be excused?"

"You hardly ate a thing." Sally looked worried. "But sure," she added before Dad could object, "go on and have a look around."

It was strange, Martha thought, how even with all these lamps on around the house, everything was still so dark. She felt hopelessly disoriented — like a mouse in a maze — silent walls rising around her, high ceilings and hidden corners swarming with shadows. She hated this house. *Hated* it. She'd never liked scary things. She'd never understood Dad's macabre sense of humor or his fascination with the unknown, or the articles he was always researching and writing for those dumb human interest magazines. And she hated *herself* — it was horrible being sixteen and such a baby.

But it's not you this time . . . it's this house.

Martha raised her eyes, her gaze settling on the heavy draperies at the far end of the hall.

Just now . . . she was sure she'd seen them move.

Just a slight rise . . . a fall . . . as if they were alive . . . breathing . . . as if someone might be hiding just behind the dingy folds of velvet. . . .

She stared at them, mesmerized. She felt her feet moving her backwards, but she couldn't turn around. . . .

She didn't see the figure standing behind her, its shadow spreading slowly over the wall.

She felt the hand against her back, and shrieking,

she spun wildly as Conor sidestepped her flailing arms.

"You!" Martha gasped. "Don't you *ever* do that to me!"

"I thought you heard me," he said calmly.

"Heard you! What are you, part ghost?" She was shaking now, as much from anger as from fear, and Conor had that look on his face that she hated so much.

"Do you want to see the rest of the house?" He started down the hall, glancing back at her over his shoulder. She stood there rigidly, glaring at him. "I wouldn't get too close to those curtains, if I were you. I think they're moving."

Martha caught her breath, then with forced casualness, caught up with him at the staircase.

As they wound through the house, she grew more confused by the minute. There were so many rooms — so many different hallways and stairwells — so many nooks and niches and closets that it was overwhelming and frightening. When they finally ended up in the kitchen, she collapsed in a chair with a gloomy sigh.

"I'll never find my way around this awful place."

Conor regarded her thoughtfully. "Before you know it, it'll feel like part of you."

"It'll never feel like part of me. It's *not* part of me."

Conor shrugged and helped himself to some cake on the counter. "You have to admit, it has character."

Martha stared miserably at the floor. *Character!* She couldn't believe how drastically her safe, happy world had changed — and now Dad and Sally would be so wrapped up in each other and this stupid house and its character, they'd never care how unhappy she was. And as for Conor. . . .

Martha glanced up quickly. She could have sworn he'd been watching her, his body propped lazily back against the wall, but now that she looked at him, his eyes were on the doorway where Sally was peeking in.

"I think I'll go on up; I'm really tired." Martha gave an exaggerated stretch, and Sally leaned down to hug her.

"I'm so glad you're here, Martha. So glad we're *all* here."

Forcing a smile, Martha left the kitchen. *Everyone's glad to be here but me.* The thought made her feel lonelier than ever, and she dragged herself upstairs, fighting back tears.

The cold was still there, trapped inside her room.

Not as strong as it had been before . . . not as jolting . . . but there, just the same . . . seeping from the corners like an invisible fog. . . .

Martha rubbed her arms and began emptying her suitcases. *This room must be on the windy side of the house; that's why the temperature's so much lower.* . . . For a brief moment she toyed with the idea of telling Dad, but then decided against it. He would only joke about it or accuse her of being difficult. *I'm just tired . . once I get a good night's sleep, it'll be gone . . . once the sun comes out I'll probably even laugh at myself.* She hoped Conor wouldn't say anything about it — she'd been embarrassed enough, acting like such an idiot in front of him.

Shutting her door, Martha got into her nightgown, her eyes going uneasily across the room . . . the windows . . . the closet. *Funny . . . that closet was open before. . . .* Puzzled, she tried to remember — had Conor closed it when he'd shown her around earlier? She was almost positive he hadn't, yet now the door was shut.

Beads of sweat prickled her forehead. It was so quiet . . . so lonely. . . . She couldn't hear anyone talking downstairs. Maybe they'd all gone out somewhere. . . . Maybe she was completely alone. . . .

With a cry, Martha jerked open the closet door.

The closet was empty.

Weak-kneed, she crawled into bed, leaving the lamp on beside her pillow. Just this once I'll keep it on, she argued with herself, *just this first night and I don't care if they do laugh at me. . . .*

Exhaustion settled over her like a huge weight. She was asleep almost at once, deep and dreamless, and she had no idea how long it had been, how many hours she'd lain there, when the phone jarred her awake.

Martha bolted upright, heart pounding, eyes frantically probing the darkness as she fought to remember where she was. The lamp was out, and beyond her door the phone shrilled again, insistent.

"Dad?" Martha called out fuzzily. "Sally?"

Stumbling out into the hall, Martha felt her way towards the sound. Someone had left a nightlight burning near the baseboard, and it cast a pool of shadows at her feet.

"Dad?" Martha tried again, and her hand fumbled for the receiver, rattling it off the cradle, its scream abruptly silenced.

"Hello?" Martha mumbled.

And at first there was nothing.

At first the quiet was so convincing that Martha really thought it had been a mistake and the embarrassed caller had hung up.

And then she heard the breathing.

Slow . . . hollow. . . .

The raspy, choking sound it made as it tried to speak. . . .

"Look outside," it whispered. *"Trick or treat."*

Martha dropped the phone. As her heart hammered in her throat, she groped back through the darkness to her room. *It's just a crank call . . . what's the matter with you? You've gotten crank calls before. . . .*

But her window was there, waiting for her as she walked in, a black gaping hole against the night, frenzied trees clawing at the glass. . . .

Martha moved across the floor like someone in a bad dream. She climbed onto the window seat and forced herself to look out.

The body was hanging there, so close she could have touched him.

14

She knew he was dead from the way he was swinging, a slow, crazy dance in the cold, cold wind.

There was a carving knife through his head. . . .

And as the moonlight fell across his slashed face, he grinned up at her.

Chapter 2

As Martha screamed, a pair of hands came out of nowhere, catching her by the shoulders.

"What is it?" Conor's face was eerily distorted in the half light. As Martha shrank back from him, he pressed his face to the glass, stared a moment, then steered her to the side of her bed. "It's the scarecrow."

"What!"

"The one from the porch. Someone sure went to a lot of trouble for a joke."

Martha wrapped her arms around herself. "Where's Dad?"

"They couldn't sleep. They went for a drive." He squatted down on the floor in front of her. "What happened?"

"It was *horrible*!" Martha buried her face in her hands. "Didn't you hear it ringing? The phone call — what he said — "

"Who?"

"I don't know!"

"*What*, then? Talk to me."

"A man, I think — I don't *know* — the voice was deep. Kind of . . . throaty — "

"Throaty." Conor nodded, mouthing the word again to himself.

"Like he needed to clear his throat — like he was having trouble getting air . . . sort of choking. He told me to look outside. And then he said 'Trick or Treat.' "

"Trick or treat." Conor stared hard at the floor.

"What is it? What are you thinking?" Martha tensed.

"I'm thinking . . . what a fool he is — it's not even Halloween yet."

"Stop making fun of me!"

"I'm not making fun of you. Why would I make fun of you?"

She saw the look then — Conor's look — creeping slowly across his face, and she shook her head, too upset to argue. Conor crossed to the window again and stared out into the night. He wasn't wearing a shirt, just rumpled jeans. He ran one hand through his thick, tawny hair.

"I'll get rid of that thing in the morning. And if the phone rings again, don't answer it. Let *me* answer it. It's probably just kids being cute, but don't answer it anyway."

Martha shut her eyes. "It just figures."

"What does?"

"That something else would happen in this *stupid* house. I don't know why your mother ever picked it out to begin with."

"Well," Conor mulled it over, "I guess because

she was trying to please your father."

Martha looked daggers at him. "Dad was pleased in Chicago."

This time Conor turned around, leveling a stare straight at her. "You're really having a problem with their happiness, aren't you?"

"I — what! Don't you tell me what I feel!"

He nodded. "Okay, then, here's the scenario. Two lonely people find each other and have a brand-new chance at life. Enter, one spoiled brat who — "

"Get out," Martha snapped. "Just get out of my room."

"The room where something terrible happened." He gave a smile. "You." He just managed to duck out the door as Martha's purse crashed into the wall, missing his head but spilling its contents all over the floor.

For a long time she huddled there, trying not to think about the phone call — trying not to look at the window. That breathing . . : "Trick or treat. . . ." But of course Conor had to be right — with Halloween coming up, it was only natural for kids to play jokes — especially on the new people in town. A prank, that's all it was. But as Martha slid back beneath the covers she couldn't shake her feeling of dread. That sense of tragedy was still lurking here in the room . . . just at the edge of her senses . . . wrapped up in the cold. . . .

It seemed she had scarcely dozed off before she woke again, this time to gray daylight and the far-away sound of thunder. Great, Martha thought, sound effects to match the house. She peered timidly from the window, but the scarecrow was gone. Pulling on jeans and a sweatshirt, she followed the smell of burnt bacon down to the kitchen.

"Martha! Isn't it a glorious day!" Sally looked up from a counterful of dirty pots and pans and smiled out at the threatening rain clouds. "Did you sleep well?"

So Conor hadn't said anything about last night. Martha felt strangely relieved. "I was really tired. Where's Conor?"

"I think he's filling the wood box out back." As Sally waved her spoon, a yellow sauce glopped all over the floor. Martha sidestepped it and tried not to shudder. "Breakfast is nearly done — will you tell him?"

"Sure." Martha secretly wondered how Conor had managed to grow so tall and healthy on his mother's cooking, and the thought almost made her laugh.

A damp wind blew across the back stoop, and Martha stood there, shivering. Trees crowded close on all sides, and the tiny yard was choked with weeds and dead leaves. For the first time, she was keenly aware of just how isolated they really were.

There was a subtle movement at the edge of the clearing, and Conor stepped out from the woods, his arms stacked with logs. Martha waited while he came up onto the porch and dropped them into a box by the door. He brushed his hands together and smiled off towards the tangled treeline.

"It's nice back in there. You can hear the forest just living around you."

Martha followed his eyes, seeing nothing but bare brown ugliness. "I don't hear anything. It's so . . . empty."

"Ummm. You're just not listening." He stepped off the porch and flexed his arms. After a minute Martha stepped down beside him.

"You didn't tell them about last night."

"Did you want me to?"

Martha studied his face, the deep blue of his eyes. "Dad probably would have laughed. He thinks I imagine things."

"Yes, I got that feeling."

"But I don't. Imagine things, I mean."

The hint of a smile came to life behind his eyes. "I know."

"Well . . . Sally said we're ready to eat."

Conor rolled his eyes and put one hand protectively to his stomach. "It's the country air. It always makes her adventurous." And then, at Martha's surprised look: "Don't worry. This phase, too, will pass." He went into the kitchen, leaving Martha to stare after him.

The moving van arrived shortly after three. For the rest of the afternoon Martha was too busy carrying and unpacking boxes to worry about anything else. Although the house began to take on some semblance of normalcy, Martha couldn't seem to make her own room any more appealing, even with all her old familiar things. Frustrated with her wasted efforts, she finally gave up and found Conor lounging against one of the columns on the front porch.

"What's the verdict?" he asked without looking up. "Think you'll stay a while?"

"Do I have a choice?"

His eyes lifted, touched her face. She thought she saw a twinkle there, but she couldn't be sure.

"If I had a choice, I'd — " She broke off as Dad stuck his head out the door and tossed his keys at them.

"Would you mind going for picture hooks? We're having a crisis in here."

Conor nodded and started towards the station wagon.

"Why don't you take Martha along?" Dad added. "Show her the town."

"If she wants."

Martha didn't relish the idea of being with Conor, but at least it was a way to get out of the house. She just managed to scramble in as the car started down the drive.

Now Martha could see the route they'd come last night — dirt road, dense woods, the endless sweep of spent fields beneath a leaden sky. She wondered how Sally had even found this place at all.

"Have you been to town a lot?" She glanced at Conor's profile, the frayed collar of his blue flannel shirt.

"Twice maybe. Don't get your hopes up — it's not Chicago."

"What about the people?"

"What about them?"

"Well, are they friendly?"

His shoulders moved lazily. "I don't know. Nobody talked to me."

She couldn't tell if he was teasing or not. For the rest of the ride she kept her attention on the bleak landscape and made breath patterns on the window. They drove for nearly twenty minutes before Conor finally turned onto another road, this one taking them past neat frame houses and well-tended yards and quiet sidewalks littered with colorful leaves. From nearly every house, jack-o'-lanterns grinned back at them, and windows were papered with skeletons, witches, and ghosts.

"Where is everyone?" The deserted streets were growing long with shadows, and Martha frowned.

Conor kept his eyes on the road. "Sensible people are fixing their dinners now — preferably something edible. Not looking for picture hooks."

"And where are we going to find these picture hooks?"

Conor swerved neatly into a parking lot and switched off the ignition. "Hardware store."

While Conor hunted along dusty counters, Martha wandered up and down the aisles, wondering if the rest of the town was as outdated as this shop. Other than a man at the register and a girl on a ladder at the back of the store, she and Conor seemed to be the only people around. She spied an old mirror propped on a shelf, and leaned close to inspect its dingy glass. And then she saw the smeared reflection above her shoulder, and she froze.

She hadn't heard anyone walk up, but the boy was right behind her, his body rigid, his dark eyes wide, an expression of pure shock locking his handsome features in place. Alarmed, Martha spun to face him, but as his gaze bored into her, he seemed to mentally shake himself, and he stepped back. Now, Martha realized, all he looked was incredibly embarrassed.

"Sorry — " he stammered. "From the back . . . I mean . . . I thought you were someone else. Hey, I'm really sorry. Are you finding what you need?"

"I . . ." He was still staring, and Martha felt her cheeks beginning to burn. The boy's smile widened, warm and genuine.

"Picture hooks, Martha. They're called picture hooks, remember?" Conor hissed. He appeared out of nowhere, sighed, and shook his head at her. Martha turned even redder.

"Hooks? Sure, back in that corner — hey, Wynn!" the boy yelled, and the girl on the ladder climbed down. "Find some picture hooks, will you?"

Martha glanced back to see the girl studying her, but the boy repeated his request, more urgently this time, and the girl hurried into a back room. The boy's eyes settled back on Martha and stayed there, politely curious.

"I haven't seen you around, have I?"

Conor made a noise in his throat and walked away. Martha wanted to die.

"No . . . I mean, you couldn't have . . . I mean, I haven't been here." *Straighten up, Martha!* "What I mean is, I just got here." *Brilliant. What a profound statement.*

"To town?" His smile was so wonderful that Martha couldn't help smiling back. "You mean you just moved here?"

"Yes," Martha brightened. "Yesterday. Sort of."

"Sort of?" He laughed, and his eyes flicked down her body to her feet and back again. "I'm Blake Chambers."

"Martha Stevenson." She stuck her hand out awkwardly, and his fingers closed around it. "Nice to meet you. In fact, you're the first person I've met here."

"Great, then I'll be the official welcome committee. So where do you live, anyway? I don't remember any houses being for sale around town."

"Well, we're not really in town." Martha brushed self-consciously at a stray wisp of hair. "It's a big old house — sort of out in the country. I don't really know my way around yet, but. . . ." Her voice trailed off as his smile faded then seemed to recover itself. For one crazy instant she could almost have sworn he looked frightened.

"Not the old Bedford place?"

Martha shook her head. "I don't know. I didn't know it had a name."

But his smile was back again, warm and irresistible. "Sure. Everyone knows the old Bedford house. I'd say your work's cut out for you." He glanced back at Conor, who was sorting through a shoebox the girl held for him. "Your boyfriend?"

"Who, Conor?" Martha spun around, flustered. "No — he's . . . he's — "

"I know," Blake teased. "You're just good friends."

Friends, thought Martha ironically, we're not even that. But aloud she said, "Our parents just got married. To each other, I mean." *God, Martha, could you sound any stupider?*

"Wow. New family. New town. That's really tough."

"Oh . . . well . . . it's okay." Martha gave a shy smile. "Do you work here?"

"Not if I can help it." His laugh was easy. "My uncle owns the place — Wynn back there, she's my cousin. I'm just helping out today."

Martha nodded and tried to think of something to say, but Blake saved her.

"Look, I've gotta get out of here — I'm late already. Nice meeting you — I'll probably see you at school, huh?"

"I hope so." Martha bit her lip. *Nothing like begging.* She watched him say good-bye to the man at the register as he shot out the door. A moment later a car squealed out of the parking lot. *I'll bet it's a date he's late for . . . with a beautiful girl. . . .*

"He's not your type," Conor said.

Martha jumped, her face flaming. He looked down at her and slowly shook his head. "Too late. You're entranced."

"Mind your own business." Martha shouldered

past him to the car and refused to say another word all the way home. Not that it mattered, she thought ruefully — Conor didn't say a word to her, either, and seemed to enjoy the quiet.

But at least Blake was something new to think about — something to keep her mind off her miserable predicament. As soon as she could, Martha excused herself from another disastrous dinner and went outside. The rain that had threatened all day now hung in a thick mist, blurring the outlines of the trees, muffling the world in gray. She walked slowly around the house, shivering in the dampness. Through a veiled sky the moon struggled up through tangled trees, its feeble light tossed by the wind. *"The old Bedford place. . . ."*

Frowning, she remembered that stricken look on Blake's face . . . how he'd mistaken her for someone else. . . . Throwing a look back over her shoulder, Martha tensed at a clammy blast of cold wind. The trees rustled, limbs flailing like scrawny arms. She came to an abrupt halt at the back corner of the house and looked off into the woods.

And then she felt her skin crawl.

Something back there was moving.

With a gasp, she stared hard at the tree line, her mind confused. There was nothing there but darkness — tight, packed darkness — and yet somehow — *somehow* — she knew something was back there — unseen — unheard — just watching. . . .

"There's supposed to be an old cemetery somewhere on the property. . . ."

As Martha stared wide-eyed at the throbbing

darkness, such an awful terror seized her that she thought she might be sick.

And then she heard the sound.

The crying.

So softly at first, that she thought it was the wind whining around the eaves of the old house . . . sighing through the dead, dead trees — only it was so sad . . . so pathetic . . . that suddenly Martha's head was full of it, the heartbreaking crying that came from nowhere and wouldn't stop —

"Who's there?" she called. "Is someone there?" And the mist was so thick that she couldn't see the house anymore, or the sky, and the wind was whipping around her, echoing through the trees — louder . . . and louder . . . not like crying now . . . like breathing. . . .

It *was* breathing.

Martha went rigid, her heart threatening to explode. It was *everywhere* now — *everywhere* — behind her and around her and there just in front of her where something watched, where something waited in the dark —

"Oh, God," Martha whispered. "Oh — "

And she stood there, too terrified to move, and the trees shuddered as something shifted deep within their shadows —

And slipped away.

She felt it the second it happened.

As the mist curled silently around her, Martha felt the sudden yawning emptiness where something had just been, there before her in the night.

And finally, she was able to run.

Chapter 3

"You're not taking this very well." Conor rested his elbow on the open window and relaxed his other hand on the steering wheel.

"How should I take it? Jump for joy?" Martha banged her head back against the seat and closed her eyes. "I can't believe it. Two days here and the magazine needs him on assignment."

"He's very excited about it."

"Of course he is. Sally's going with him, and they'll have a fine vacation."

"Honeymoon," Conor corrected. "We're the ones who get the vacation."

"From what?" Martha grumbled.

"Mom's cooking."

Martha glanced at him, almost wanting to laugh, but too upset to give him the satisfaction. Instead she slumped even lower in her seat, her mind in a dark, ugly whirl. She hadn't told anyone about what had happened to her last night. By the time she'd raced back to the house, the phone call had come, and Dad had been too ecstatic to listen to anything, and she'd shut herself in her room to cry. How could Dad and Sally even *think* about taking a honeymoon now — even if Dad *was* on assignment in Hawaii? How could they even *think* of leaving her alone in that creepy old house with Conor and some horrible thing running loose in the woods! *I'll never forgive them, I'll —*

"I'll meet you back here at the car after school," Conor said, and Martha sat up with a start, surprised that they were already in the student lot. The school looked quaint and comfortable — and small, Martha thought — but as she scanned the groups of kids hurrying across campus she felt sick. "You should have eaten something." Conor was looking at her, and Martha shoved herself out onto the pavement.

"I'm fine. I don't need you to worry about me."

"I know." That hint of a smile again. "You don't need anybody."

Martha bit her lip and followed him into the first brick building, down a wide, noisy hall, and into an office. Before she could even think what to do, Conor had spoken to a secretary, and within minutes she found herself in an even tinier office, facing her new advisor across a cluttered desk.

"Martha Stevenson? I'm Greg Chambers. *Mister* Chambers in the halls and in class, but Greg's fine in here. Welcome to Bedford High."

As Martha felt her hand enclosed in his warm grasp, she tried not to stare — not only was Greg Chambers boyishly handsome, but she also had the feeling they'd met before.

"I know things are going to be all new and different for you here — *and* at home." As she glanced up, a smile broke his perfectly tanned face. "Your stepmother's been to see me and explained the situation, of course. It's rough, I know — I come from a broken home myself. So give yourself time — and permission. Feel all the things you want to feel, and they'll be easier to handle if you do."

He spoke so casually that Martha felt herself relaxing. She nodded, allowing herself a long, hard assessment as he flipped through a folder. He couldn't have been that old, she told herself — maybe mid- to late-twenties, with dark hair and eyes and a tall, well-built frame. She fixed her eyes on the back of his head and frowned. *Someone . . . he reminds me of someone. . . .*

"Blake!" she burst out. "Blake Chambers!"

He spun around, startled. "You know Blake?"

"No . . . I mean . . . I met him in the hardware store yesterday."

"Well, I knew Blake worked fast but — hey, don't look like that, I'm kidding! He's my cousin. The *famous* one."

"Famous?"

"Oh, so you really haven't gotten the whole charm treatment, huh?" Greg chuckled and slid back down into his chair. "Athlete extraordinaire — leading scorer on the basketball team — top high-jumper in the state — of course, I *am* prejudiced. Not to mention extremely jealous."

Martha laughed at that. "Did you go to school here?"

"Where else?" Greg leaned back in his chair, waving his arms in an inclusive gesture. "I loved it here. Loved the town. Still do." He gazed at her, noting how her expression fell, then he bent forward. "Give it a chance, Martha. It's not the big city, but it's got its own kind of charm — its own kind of excitement. We're all here to help you. Especially me."

Martha nodded grudgingly, forcing a smile.

"Okay. Now let's decide where to put you. I hear you're quite the writer. Awards in state competition — yearbook — school paper — "

In spite of herself, Martha smiled. "They were just little awards. I have a lot to learn."

"Great. Then let's start with my creative writing class. I'm pretty fascinating."

Martha couldn't help laughing. "Do I have to try out?"

"With your qualifications — are you kidding? Hey, don't look so worried. You'll love it."

He was right, and as the day wore on, that class turned out to be the only thing Martha *did* love. Sitting through each new hour was torturous; she could feel all the kids staring at her with unabashed curiosity. At lunchtime no one asked her to eat with them, but she could see heads together and fingers pointing as they talked about her. She didn't see Conor all day, and by the time school was finally over, she felt so lonely that even *he* was beginning to sound good to her. "I'm a sick person," she mumbled to herself, and didn't realize that someone had come up beside her locker.

"Hi, remember me? I saw you in the store yesterday." The girl was smiling shyly, peering at Martha over an armload of books.

Martha smiled back at her, amused. Even if she hadn't remembered, the girl's uncanny resemblance to Blake and Greg Chambers was a dead giveaway.

"We have writing class together," the girl went on hesitantly. "I tried to get your attention, but you were a million miles away."

"Oh . . . sorry," Martha stammered. "I'm kind of in a fog today, I guess."

"I would be, too. In fact, I'd be even worse." The girl nodded solemnly, then offered another smile. "I'm Wynn Chambers."

In spite of her weariness, Martha laughed. "How many more of you are there around here?" For a moment Wynn looked confused, and Martha laughed again. "Besides you and Blake and my new advisor?"

This time Wynn laughed, too, tossing back her long brown hair with a shake of her head. "Is Greg your advisor? I'm glad — you'll like him." She was tall like her cousins, with the same quick, wide smile, and the same merry brown eyes.

"I like him already. In fact, he was the high point of my day."

"Oh . . . that bad, huh?" Wynn looked sympathetic, like she truly understood. A group of girls jostled past, calling her name; she waved and turned back to Martha. "Isn't Bedford what you expected?"

"Well. . . ." Martha stared for a moment into her locker, taking a quick inventory of what she'd need for homework. "To tell the truth, I didn't even know I was coming here, so I didn't know what to expect. I just woke up one morning and found out everything had changed."

"That would make me sad." Wynn looked down at the floor, nodding her head. "I don't like changes. Changes are scary."

Martha stared at her a moment, then smiled. "You're right. It really *is* scary." She closed her locker and swung her purse to her other shoulder. "Do you live here in town?"

"Four blocks from here. Blake lives another block from me, and Greg's mom still lives in the house behind that."

"Uh-oh. What happened to poor Greg?"

Wynn giggled. "He has an apartment on the other side of town. Do you have brothers and sisters?"

Martha shook her head, giving a wry smile. "I didn't. But now I have this weird stepbrother named Conor — he's going to school here, too — "

Wynn glanced at her, eyes widening. "Conor? The Conor you were with at the store?"

"Yes, that's him. Why?"

"I can't believe he's your brother." Wynn was suddenly looking shy again.

"*Step*brother."

"You haven't noticed how everyone's been lusting after him?"

"Lusting after Conor!" Martha fell into step beside her.

"Well, they have. All the *girls* have." Wynn

flushed slightly and added, "Heads have been turning since he got here. Like the domino effect every time he walks down the hall. They haven't been able to keep their eyes off him."

"Conor?" Martha groaned and shoved the door open, glad to be outside at last. Leave it to Conor, she thought dismally. *I get treated like a plague victim, and all the girls in school have fallen in love with him.*

"But he's . . . he seems kind of different, doesn't he?" Wynn chose her words cautiously.

"He's different, all right."

"He hardly looks at anyone. I'll bet he doesn't even know how all the girls are staring."

"He knows." Martha shot her a look, and they turned out of the gate to the parking lot. "There's Conor now. Do you want to meet him officially?" *Oh, please let me introduce you to the hottest new sex symbol at Bedford High. . . .*

Wynn stopped, clutching her books to her chest. "I . . . I should be getting home."

She's nervous about meeting Conor, about actually seeing him up close again, face to face. . . . "Come on," Martha encouraged. "I know he'll remember you from yesterday. You could come to my house and we could — "

"No." Wynn shook her head, looking embarrassed. "I . . . maybe another time."

"Well, sure, whenever you want — "

"Hey, Wynn! Martha! Wait up, will you?"

Martha felt her heart skip as Blake Chambers

came running towards them from the gym, his body long and leanly muscled, his hair still damp from the showers. He caught Wynn in a huge hug, nearly knocking her down, and fixed his eyes on Martha with a grin.

"How's it going? You survive the first day without too many battle scars?"

"Barely." Martha's pulse quickened as he came over and took three of her books, his arm brushing hers as he leafed through the pages.

"Hmmm . . . I seem to remember all this horrible stuff . . . don't tell me you like Poe?"

"It doesn't matter whether we like him or not; we still have to read him," Wynn sighed. "But guess what? Martha's in Greg's writing class with me — "

"Great. So what are you writing?"

"Typical Greg. He gave us some corny assignment for Halloween — "

"And speak of the devil — come on, let's catch a ride. See you later, huh, Martha?" As Blake loped off, Wynn glanced openmouthed at Martha, then both girls began to laugh.

"He's not always this rude," Wynn apologized. "Greg must be in a hurry."

"Greg?"

"Yes, see? Over there — the red Jaguar."

Martha squinted against the crisp breeze. "I can't believe how much alike Blake and Greg look. You, too, for that matter."

"It's just 'cause I'm tall," Wynn said ruefully. "I hate being tall. No one asks you out when you're tall." She shrugged. "Everybody says we look alike. Blake and Greg especially. They almost look like brothers."

"From a distance they could be twins."

They were almost to the station wagon now. Martha could see Conor inside and she stopped, wondering if Wynn would change her mind about saying hello.

"I'll see you tomorrow." Wynn stopped abruptly, tugging her sweater around her. "It'll get better — just think — your first day's over and you're not new anymore."

"That's easy for you to say," Martha chuckled. "I'm stuck right in the middle of every class, and I have tons to catch up on — even our writing assignment sounds hard."

Wynn looked surprised. "What? Writing a ghost story for Halloween? That shouldn't be any problem — especially for you."

Martha was doubtful. "Just 'cause my dad's a writer, that doesn't mean any of his talent rubbed off on me."

"Your father's a writer? I didn't know that."

"You didn't? I thought that's what you meant — "

"I didn't know about your father," Wynn said. "I was talking about . . . well, *you* know. About your house."

Martha stared at her. Something about the way Wynn was looking back at her made her uneasy. "What . . . about my house?"

"Hey, Wynn!" Blake yelled. The Jaguar was moving slowly towards them, and Blake was hanging out the window. "Hurry up! Greg's got a meeting!"

Wynn wasn't even listening to him; her expression was on Martha, and it looked suddenly strained. "You . . . really don't know, do you? Nobody told you — "

Martha shook her head. "Are you talking about the old cemetery?"

And Wynn was looking so strange — sort of sad and sympathetic at the same time, and Martha took a step back, not wanting to hear any more —

"There was a murder in your house," Wynn said quietly. "Everyone knows the old Bedford place is evil."

Chapter 4

"Evil?" Conor glanced over at Martha as he eased the car into a curve. She was staring rigidly out at the road, her hands locked in her lap.

"That's what she said," Martha insisted. "She said everyone knows about it. But obviously nobody told us."

"They wouldn't, would they?" Conor said reasonably. "The realtor'd be afraid of losing a good sale."

"We've been tricked," Martha said. "I feel like everyone's laughing at us."

"No one tricked us. And if somebody thinks they did, the joke's on them. If your dad had known it was evil, he'd have snapped it up even faster."

Martha knew Conor was right — but the memory of school still hurt. "No wonder people kept looking at me like I had three heads," she mumbled. She waited for Conor to make some joke, but when he didn't, she chanced a quick look in his direction. He was staring at her, deep in thought.

"Nobody's laughing at us," he said at last. "If

anything, it makes us irresistibly interesting."

"Like freaks. Wait till I tell Dad about — " She broke off, remembering that she wouldn't even see him for several weeks. The thought made her feel defeated somehow, and she slumped in her seat.

"So what happened in our infamous house to make it so evil?" Conor asked quietly.

"A murder. That's all I know. Wynn had to hurry to catch a ride with Greg, and that's all she said."

"Who's Greg?"

"My advisor. Mr. Chambers. Did you know they're all cousins — Greg and Wynn and Blake?" She deliberately kept her eyes averted. "He's the guy in the hardware store yesterday — "

"Of course. How could I forget Blake Chambers?"

Martha ignored him. "Well, anyway, Wynn and I have class together — she's the one who was on the ladder in the store. I really like her."

"So do we at least know who or what is supposed to be making the house so evil?"

"Some ghost, I guess."

"Aah."

Martha bristled. "Look, I don't know any more about it than you do. I don't even want to talk about it anymore." She closed her eyes, fighting panicky thoughts away — the body in the tree . . . the cold in her room . . . the invisible watcher in the woods. . . . *Tell him! Tell him what happened!* "It's probably just a lie, anyway. It's probably something that got started, and it's not even true. Don't you think so?"

Conor didn't answer, so Martha stared out the window the rest of the way home. Compared to this dreary countryside, school had seemed so normal . . . so alive . . . full of noise and activity and real people. Now it was already starting to get dark, and the longer they drove, the more lonely she felt. There was nothing out here . . . *nothing*. And again, the heavy sky dripped with almost-rain, shrouding the world in gray. As they finally made the turn onto their road, Martha pulled her jacket around her like a cocoon, bracing herself for the sight of the house. As soon as Conor parked the car she ran inside and up to her room.

Oh, God, I can't stand this! Weeks in this hideous place with only Conor to keep her company! Martha threw herself across her bed and lay there, drained. How could life get any worse? If Conor only knew about what had happened near the woods last night, he wouldn't be nearly so unconcerned about the evil house stories. *Then why don't you tell him? 'Cause he'd never believe me. I don't have any kind of proof. In fact, I'm not even sure anymore that I believe it myself. . . .*

Martha groaned and went to the window, rubbing her arms against the nagging chill. She couldn't even relax in this room — no matter what she did to it, she just couldn't seem to make it comfortable. She stared down into the backyard and was startled to see Conor go into the woods. *Now what is he doing down there?*

The thought of being in the house alone wasn't a pleasant one. Before Martha even realized what she was doing, she was standing on the back porch, staring off towards the trees where she'd seen him disappear.

"Conor!"

Her voice came to her eerily on the wind, as if the trees had caught it in their twisted arms and thrown it back. There was no other sound, though Martha held her breath, straining to hear. Heavy rain clouds still hung stubbornly in the sky, making the air unbearably clammy. She hunched her shoulders and started resolutely across the yard.

"Conor! Where are you?"

But she might as well have been the only living person in the world, the evening lay so gray and empty around her. Nervously Martha glanced behind her at the house. Only one light was visible through the half-open curtains of the kitchen; the rest of the rooms stood lifelessly behind blank windows. Cautiously she tried to peer through the trees, then parted a web of branches and saw a narrow path beyond. "Conor, I know you're in there — I saw you from the window!"

What is he doing in there?

Martha moved deeper into the trees, deeper into the thickening dusk, her thoughts whirling. Was this where she'd seen the movement last night? Right about here? In her fear, in the dark, it was impossible to remember the exact spot. . . . Drawing a shaky breath she stopped, confused. Suddenly she was afraid to go on. Afraid to go on and afraid to go back. *What if it's still here? Watching me . . . even now —*

"Martha — "

Martha screamed and collapsed against a tree, her hand to her heart. *"Conor!* Where *were* you? I couldn't — "

"What are you doing following me around without a jacket?" he said, as if nothing was out of the ordinary.

"I wasn't following you around — I was — "

"And if you get pneumonia, I'll get blamed for it."

"Why should *you* get blamed for it?"

"Because I'm supposed to be looking after you, that's why." He set his jaw and began shrugging out of his jacket.

Martha drew herself up indignantly. "Looking after me! I beg your pardon, but — "

"Yeah, I know." Conor bundled her into his jacket as if she were a sack of potatoes. "You don't need looking after; you can take care of yourself. Zip that up and come on."

"Why?" Martha asked suspiciously. "Where are we going?"

"I want to show you something." He took off through the trees before she could respond, and she had no choice but to follow him.

The air was sharp and wet in her lungs. As Conor's long legs moved him effortlessly ahead of her, Martha found it harder and harder to breathe and keep up. The pathway had long since disappeared beneath a carpet of leaves, yet Conor seemed to know the way. Every so often, Martha noticed, he would pause, tilting his face into the wind as if listening for some direction she was unable to hear. And as they wove their way deeper and deeper into the murky forest, Martha's apprehension grew until the tight band around her heart was as much from fear as from cold.

"Conor, where are we — ?"

"Look."

He stopped abruptly, bent low beneath a knotted overhang of branches, and as Martha stumbled up beside him, his arm went around her shoulders. Wedged against him, Martha stared where he was pointing, the icy cold creeping all through her body.

The cemetery lay before them like the ruins of some ghostly garden, headstones toppled and staggered across the leaf-strewn ground. Where shrubs and vines had once flowered, now there were only masses of brown stems, and the low-sweeping trees looked grossly misshapen in the fast-falling twilight. A light fog had begun to snake among the headstones and old, crumbling statues stared back at the intruders through stone eyes. Martha took it all in, not even aware of how she was pressing back against Conor. She felt him squeeze her shoulders and give her a slight turn, and as her eyes fell upon the magnificent stone structure at the far end of the cemetery, she wondered crazily if she could possibly be dreaming.

"What is that?" she gasped.

"It's a mausoleum. Come on."

"No — wait — " But he strode off again, pulling her along, and Martha's eyes stayed glued to the huge tomb as they came up beside it.

"Conor — please — let's get out of here — "

"Look at the inscription." Conor let go of her at last, and pointed to the foot-high letters carved in the black stone wall. The tomb itself had to be at least twenty feet tall and equally as wide, but its double doors were barred by thick iron gates which looked like they hadn't been opened in many, many years. "Isn't Bedford supposed to be the name of our house?" He glanced back to see Martha nodding. "They must have been pretty important. It's the fanciest grave in the whole place."

Martha pulled his jacket tightly around her, and glanced back nervously over her shoulder. "How did you ever find this place? Have you been looking for it all this time?"

For several moments he didn't answer. He planted his feet firmly apart on the ground, his body braced against the wind as he stared up at the Bedford name. Watching him, Martha was seized with a violent trembling — he could almost have been one of the lifeless statues keeping vigil around them.

"No, I haven't been looking for it," he said quietly.

"Then what? You found it by accident, getting wood?"

"No. I never came this far."

He had such a strange look on his face. Martha felt her knees weaken, and she leaned back against a tree.

"It was so strong," Conor murmured, more to himself than to her. He glanced back at her, a look so puzzled that suddenly Martha was angry.

"*Damn* you, Conor — why did you bring me here? If you think you can scare me, it won't — "

He reached out for the doors, as if to shake them, then his hand froze, a slow stiffening creeping over his body.

"Conor — what *is* it?"

And as she stared at his outstretched hand, Martha felt an irrational rush of terror through her heart.

"Conor — let's go back — please!" She hadn't even realized that she'd grabbed his arm, and now as she tried to turn him around, he looked down at her, remotely amused.

"You're pretty strong for being so little."

"Conor, I mean it — this isn't a bit funny — "

Nodding, he reached down and gently pried her fingers from his arm. "Let's go back to the house. It's gone now, anyway."

"What's gone?"

"Nothing. Never mind." He backed away from the tomb and began striding off rapidly towards the trees.

"We'll never find our way back!" Martha's voice rose anxiously. "It all looks alike out here — we don't even have a light — "

"Trust me," Conor said. "I know the way."

Martha didn't argue. She took off after him, keeping close behind, amazed that he could make any sense at all of their hopelessly tangled surroundings. When they reached the house at last, she sank gratefully into a kitchen chair, laying her head down on the table, watching as Conor busied himself at the stove, making omelettes.

"I'm not hungry," Martha said.

"Give me a break. I'm a great cook."

She gave a long sigh and pulled slowly out of his jacket. "It's getting worse. It's just getting worse and worse every minute."

"What is?"

"This." Martha threw up her arms. "All this — this house — and — and — everything about it. Now you."

"What about me?"

"I knew you were weird before. But tonight was a classic. Do you want to tell me what happened out there?"

"Nothing happened." He avoided her eyes. "I just thought you'd enjoy sightseeing by twilight, that's all."

"Yeah, right. Conor, don't treat me like I don't have a brain — and don't *look* at me like that — I *hate* when you look at me with that look — "

"What look?"

"It's a conspiracy, isn't it?" Martha glared. "Something you and Dad dreamed up before he left, just to have fun with me."

"You don't look like you're having much fun," Conor said.

"I can't stand this. I just can't." Martha pushed herself up and tossed his jacket at him. Conor caught it neatly, without even turning around. "Oh, fine. Great. I'm going to bed. I need to rest my overactive imagination."

She went to her room and turned her TV on as loud as she could stand it. The noise brought little comfort, however, and she lay across her bed, thumbing through her books, making a halfhearted stab at her homework. But her thoughts weren't on school. Her thoughts were on that huge monument in the woods and Conor's strange behavior, and on what Wynn had said as she'd left her that afternoon:

"Everyone knows the old Bedford place is evil. . . ."

Martha stared at the wall, her schoolwork forgotten. What had happened here to make people talk? To make people afraid? What horrible thing had gone on inside these walls? Did it have something to do with the old cemetery . . . or the hidden watcher in the woods. . . .

Troubled, she climbed into bed and lay there in the dark, her eyes riveted on the shadows beneath her window. *Why didn't you tell him? Why didn't you tell him about the something watching you?* Yet she knew why. Because maybe she really *had* imagined it. And maybe . . . if she never said it out loud . . . then it could never, ever be real. . . .

She wondered what Conor was doing, if he'd finished eating, if he was nearby in his own room. She couldn't hear him moving around anywhere — only the house shifting . . . sighing in the wind . . . whispering its secrets . . . lulling her into a restless sleep. . . .

Yet even in her dreams the house was still with her . . . in deep wells of darkness she tossed and turned, vaguely aware of every creak and groan . . . every rustling. . . . On every side of her the walls were breathing . . . louder . . . louder . . . until she thought she'd scream if they didn't stop. And then they began to squeeze in . . . closer and closer . . . squeezing and creaking with every labored breath — and a deathly cold seeped from every hidden corner — and though she fought to open her eyes, a weight pressed down on her eyelids, rendering her blind and helpless. . . .

"Dad?" Martha murmured, and at last she broke through to consciousness, away from the nightmare sounds, the sighings and creakings. . . .

Except that she was wide awake now. . . .

And the creaking was still there.

Very close to her.

Here in her room.

As Martha sat up in bed, a light suddenly came on in the hall, glowing in beneath the bedroom door so that shadows went slithering off into corners. In confusion, she glanced around her room and a cry lodged in her throat.

Something was moving beside the closet.

And slowly . . . slowly . . . the half-open closet door began to close.

"Oh, no," Martha whispered, "no — "

And she didn't even realize at first that the door to the hall had opened or that Conor was throwing the covers back, pulling her from the bed.

"Hurry, Martha," he said calmly. "I smell smoke."

Chapter 5

As Martha stumbled out into the hall, Conor steered her towards the stairway and pushed her along in front of him as they raced down.

"Go outside and wait for me."

"I'm not going out there by myself!"

"Martha, don't argue — just do it."

"Conor, I can smell it! It's really strong down here!" Turning in panic, Martha pointed to the back hall. "It smells like it's there — "

Conor froze, but only for a second. "Christ," he muttered, "what's that kitchen door doing closed?"

"Conor, don't — "

"Get outside and stay there. I mean it!"

Conor's body was slamming against the kitchen door now, and as a wave of acrid smoke billowed out, Martha screamed and ran out into the yard. The chill was intense — biting through the thinness of her nightgown as she stood there shivering. Chimneys and rooftops reared their ugly heads against the night, and Martha stared back at them, terrified they would suddenly explode in clouds of smoke. *The house is burning down, I just know it.* What if the whole house suddenly collapsed right in front of her, burying Conor alive?

"Conor!" she screamed. "I'm calling the fire department!"

The door banged open and her heart nearly burst. Conor walked calmly over and tossed something at her feet.

"Don't bother. It's out."

Martha gazed down at the lump on the ground, coughing as smoke came up in her face. For a crazy moment she didn't know whether to laugh or cry.

"A dish towel! Do you mean to tell me — ?"

"It was on the stove," Conor said.

"No." Martha held up her hands. "Let me guess. On a burner that *someone* forgot to turn off."

"That's pretty good." Conor looked suitably impressed. He kicked at the charred mess and glanced up again into Martha's furious expression.

"Conor. . . ." She was so limp with relief, so shaky with anger, that she could barely speak. "I really think I could kill you right about now — "

Conor didn't seem to be listening. He was poking the smoky fabric with a stick, and his jaw was set in concentration.

"I can't believe you were so careless." Martha wouldn't let up. "We could have died in our beds! The house could have burned down around us — we could — " She broke off, looking at him in desperation. He was still staring at the dish towel, making no effort to defend himself. "Something was in my closet tonight!" she burst out.

There was a long moment of silence. Conor finally raised his eyes and looked at her. "I don't suppose it could have been a dream?"

"Could *this* have been?" Martha retorted. She took a deep shuddering breath and tried to keep from screaming at him. "Conor, you almost killed me — why should I expect you to be bothered about something hiding in my closet!"

His sigh came out wearily. "Is that what you want to believe?"

"What I want," Martha clenched her teeth as she yanked open the door, "is to get a decent night's sleep for a change!" She slammed it behind her and stomped upstairs, shutting herself in her room. But she couldn't shut out the smell of burnt cloth . . . or the soft sound of Conor's door closing hours later. And even though she forced herself to search the closet and finally barricaded it with a chair, shapeless fears haunted her dreams the rest of the night.

After another silent ride to school, she dragged herself through her classes the next morning, the lectures and discussions like meaningless blobs in her brain. The only thing she *was* aware of was how everyone still seemed to be staring at her, and she'd just decided to go off-campus for lunch when a familiar voice stopped her at her locker.

"Hey, Martha! Where've you been hiding?"

Even before she saw him, Martha's heart fluttered into her throat. A second later Blake Chambers caught her by the arm, his eyes sweeping over her approvingly as he smiled.

"You on your way to lunch?"

"Well . . . I . . ."

"Let's brave the cafeteria. Unless you have other plans."

"No, I'd really like that." *That's right, sound desperate.* She flushed as he guided her into the noisy building, straight through the crowds to a small table in the corner.

"Here we are. Just leave your things — nobody'll bother them."

Martha smiled. "Did you reserve this?"

"It's *always* reserved for me," Blake laughed, and Martha realized he was serious. *Of course it would be . . . he's the school star . . . so what on earth am I doing here?*

Martha knew she wouldn't be able to eat a thing, not with her stomach jumping around the way it was — but she didn't want to look silly and not take something. Blake stood behind her, so close she could smell the faint scent of his aftershave. He was talking about a test he'd just taken, but he might as well have been speaking a foreign language — she was so nervous, she barely heard a thing.

"What's the matter, aren't you hungry?"

Martha jumped as his lips brushed her ear. Unlike her own tray, his was crowded with food, and they were nearing the end of the line. In desperation Martha grabbed several small bowls, and they clattered onto her tray.

"Don't tell me — diet?" Blake grinned, nodding

at the pitiful lunch she'd selected. "You don't need it, Martha — not with your body."

"No, I'm not — " Martha rummaged in her purse for money. "I mean — I'm — " In dismay she watched all her change spill out onto the floor and roll in all directions. She started to bend down to retrieve it, but Blake took her by the elbow.

"Relax. My treat. You're the kind of date to take to dinner — you sure wouldn't cost much."

"Oh — I — "

"Hey, I'm kidding." He straightened, dumping a handful of retrieved coins onto her tray. "New kid in town — stomach all in knots — I wouldn't be hungry, either."

Martha managed a weak nod as he grinned at the cashier and handed over his money. When they got back to their table he sat down and regarded her with interest.

"So now that I've bored you with all my troubles, how's your day going?"

"Oh, you didn't bore me," Martha said quickly. She watched him shake a carton of milk and fill his glass. "And my day's going okay."

"Just okay, huh?" He leaned back in his chair. "I hear you've got a terrific advisor."

"Oh — Mr. Chambers." Martha smiled, twisting her napkin in her lap. "There seem to be lots of you around."

"Yeah, but Greg turned out *good*," Blake chuckled. "Not like the rest of us."

"That's not what *he* says," Martha countered.

"He's really very proud of you — I mean, he *should* be — all the things you've done and . . ." She lowered her eyes. *Great, Martha, fawn all over him, why don't you?*

Blake shrugged off the compliments. "I love sports. I'm lucky I can do what I love. That's all."

"I was never good at sports. I'm too clumsy." Martha smiled in spite of herself, and Blake leaned towards her across the table.

"You don't *look* clumsy. You look . . . what's the right word?"

Martha glanced away, her cheeks going hot. She wished he wouldn't stare at her that way . . . his eyes so dark . . . so warm. . . .

"Martha. What a surprise."

As someone touched her back, she jumped, tipping over her water. Blake grinned and rose halfway.

"Conor. Right?"

Oh, damn! Martha squirmed in her chair as Conor looked down at her, the corners of his mouth twitching.

"Blake Chambers." Blake held out his hand and Conor shook it. "Here, sit down and join us." Blake motioned to an empty chair, but Conor took a step back.

"Thanks, but I'm kind of in a hurry. Nice to meet you, though. I've heard a *lot* about you."

Martha went a deep, furious red. She put her napkin up to her face.

"Is that your lunch?" Conor asked innocently. "Since when do you eat cottage cheese?"

.Martha wished she could die. Just crawl under the table and quietly die. Blake was watching her — her and the uneaten bowls of cottage cheese on her tray.

"I always eat cottage cheese. I love cottage cheese, as a matter of fact."

"That's funny. Your dad said it makes you sick."

Martha threw him a look of pure hatred.

Conor smiled back. "See you later. Good meeting you."

"Yeah, you, too." Blake watched Conor walk off, then turned to Martha with a smile. "Seems like a nice guy. How is he as a brother?"

"*Step*brother," Martha muttered. "*Step*brother — "

"Hey, sorry!" Blake held up his hands in mock defense, and Martha finally gave in to a laugh. "Wynn says your dad's a writer."

"He writes articles mostly. Human interest stories."

"You mean two-headed alien changelings, things like that?" Blake tried to keep his expression serious.

"Not quite. Right now he's off in Hawaii on some new assignment."

Blake gave a low whistle. "I'm impressed. Too bad you couldn't go along and take notes or something."

"It's also his honeymoon," Martha sighed. "Plus, he's very strict about school."

"I can sympathize." Blake buttered a roll, and chewed thoughtfully. "My old man's a tyrant when it comes to grades. Wants me to have it better than he did — you know the old story."

"Well, it sounds like you're doing plenty to make him happy," Martha said.

Blake looked mischievous. "Hey, I enjoy winning, that's all. But you — how do you like your classes so far?"

Martha hesitated, shrugged. "They're okay, I guess. I think writing will be fun. . . ." She glanced at him, hesitating. "Can I ask you something?"

"Never on the first date." His eyes met hers with a twinkle. "Sure. Ask away."

"Our house," Martha said.

"The old Bedford place."

"Yes. Wynn said . . . well, is it really . . . evil?"

Blake leaned back in surprise. "You mean you didn't know? Nobody told you?"

Martha shook her head, frowning. "I'd really like to hear the story, if there is one."

For a minute his face seemed to struggle between sadness and uncertainty. He turned his glass slowly between his fingers. "I'm not sure you really do. Or that you really should."

"But I'm living there and it's — " She broke off, and his eyes raised slowly to her face.

"It's what?"

Martha frowned, one hand trailing across her forehead. "I . . . I can't explain it exactly. I was going to ask Wynn about it but — "

"No, don't." Blake looked at her, his expression serious, and he pushed himself back from the table.

"Don't ask Wynn. Let's go someplace where we can talk."

Martha felt uneasy as she followed him across campus. A light drizzle had discouraged much outside activity — hardly anyone seemed to be around as they walked past the buildings towards the athletic field behind school. Blake waved distractedly as several runners jogged past them on the track, then he steered Martha to the bleachers.

"Mind a little fresh air?" Blake smiled, but it seemed strained. He bowed slightly and helped her up. "Have a seat. It's been trying to rain for weeks now — when it finally comes, it probably won't stop till Christmas." He eased down beside her and leaned back, propping his elbows on the seat behind. His brown eyes searched her face. "Do you believe in ghosts, Martha?"

She wasn't quite prepared for that. As he continued to stare at her, her own eyes widened in alarm.

"I . . . what are you talking about?"

"I'm talking about your house. The Bedford house. That's what people around here believe, you know — that the tormented spirits there can't be put to rest."

"Do they really come back to the scenes of their tragedies . . . bound there forever, even in death . . . ?" Dad's words floated back to her, and Martha shook her head slowly, trying to clear it.

"Are you trying to tell me this whole *town* is superstitious about that stupid old house?"

A faint smile passed over his face. "That stupid old house has been around as long as the town. Built by the original founders. Most of the family's died out through the years, though. The last heirs put it up for sale last year."

"I can see why," Martha said wryly.

"The family was never big on updating anything — as you've probably found out by now." Blake ran one hand over the wooden seat, his brow furrowed in thought. "But the murder's not an old story. The murder just happened a year ago."

A long cold wind curled around them, rattling the bleachers. Martha glanced nervously at the sky and huddled deeper into her jacket.

"The Bedfords had money, so the house sat empty a lot. They were funny people — kind of eccentric, I guess — and Bedford was just too small for their tastes. Then George Bedford decided to move back to his roots, so he and his wife and daughter lived in the house the last few years. Elizabeth, the daughter" — his voice lowered, and for a minute Martha thought he looked sad — "Elizabeth was Wynn's age. Really pretty . . . really sweet girl. She and Wynn got to be best friends. They spent a lot of time together. The parents were pretty social — they went off to the city a lot and left Elizabeth by herself, so Wynn was good company for her."

Martha nodded, blew on her fingers, flexing her hands. "So far it doesn't sound very scary. Just sad."

"Someone murdered Elizabeth. Wynn found her at the house up in her room."

The last bit of warmth drained from Martha's body. As a soft flurry of leaves sifted down upon their shoulders, Blake reached over and untangled one from her hair. Martha flinched at his touch.

"Hey, I didn't mean to — "

"It's okay." Martha shook her head emphatically. "Go on. Please."

Blake gave an almost imperceptible nod and leaned back again, propping his feet on the seat below. "Dennis killed her," he said softly. "It was Dennis's fault."

"What . . . ?" Martha could feel her lips forming the words, but for a moment no sound would come. She watched Blake's fingers tracing the zipper of his jacket. "Who's Dennis?"

Blake shot her a meaningful look. "A guy who used to live here. I went to school with him . . . he played on the team. . . ."

"How horrible!"

"He was a total jerk. Everyone knew what a hotshot he was — he acted like he owned the whole town and he took whatever he wanted — like everyone owed him something. He wanted Elizabeth — and for a while he had her, too. Until she dumped him."

Martha was watching Blake's face, the way it was struggling to control emotions, the way his eyes averted from hers with a sudden coldness. "Why did she do that?"

" 'Cause she got smart," Blake said quickly. He stared hard into the past, the tension beginning to ease around his mouth. "I . . . I guess she just got tired of all his bullshit. He liked to brag, you know — usually about things that had never happened."

Martha nodded. "I think I get the picture. But how — ?"

Blake didn't let her finish. "I know he killed her," he said flatly. "But before he did it, he tried to put her through hell."

Another wave of gooseflesh went over her. Martha clasped her hands together tightly and pressed them against her chin, trying not to shake. "Blake . . . I — "

"You never crossed Dennis," Blake said softly. "I know . . . *everyone* knew. You never crossed him and got away with it — he'd find some way to get back . . . to make your life miserable. Everyone in town knew what he was like — he just didn't care about anything or anyone. And when Elizabeth said she didn't want to see him anymore, he made her pay for making him look bad."

Martha shook her head. "He sounds like some kind of monster."

"Oh, but he didn't look like one." Blake's laugh was derisive. "All the girls thought he was great — and he *was* good-looking. And he could turn the charm off and on like water — he was a real pro. But he didn't have any real friends. And he didn't have any loyalties. Even on the basketball team, he was a dirty player. And everyone was afraid of him, and he knew it, so that made it easy for him."

Martha was silent for a long while, her mind working to sort it all out. "And so he killed Elizabeth just to get back at her?"

"First there were the phone calls," Blake said.

Martha stared at him, an icy chill rippling up her spine. "Phone calls?" she murmured.

"Obscene phone calls. Not just kid stuff, trying to scare her. Threats." Blake's eyes closed briefly, and he ran one hand across his forehead. "He told her he'd get even with her if it was the last thing he did. He told her she'd never go out with anyone again."

"Oh, Blake — he told her *that*?"

"And he started following her. Not out in the open where she could really see him — but at a distance, just so she'd know he was there. Sometimes when he called, he'd tell her things he'd seen her do — like he'd been watching the house."

Martha was gazing at him in disbelief, her arms clenched tightly around her chest. She was beginning to feel sick, and her body was so cold now that it seemed strangely detached.

"He left a dead rat on her porch." The words came out between clenched teeth, and Blake's fist curled and uncurled again on his thigh. "And one night he set a fire — "

"A fire!" *No . . . no . . . I don't want to hear this, please stop, please. . . .*

"They caught it in time, but . . ." His voice trailed away, for one brief instant his eyes filled, but then he lifted his head, blinking defiantly. "It didn't matter in the end, did it? Nothing did. He still killed her."

Martha's throat felt thick, her words sticking with an aftertaste of fear. "But she told someone, didn't she? Why didn't the police do something?"

Blake gave a humorless smile. "That's just it. She didn't tell anyone. Not at first, anyway."

"But — but why! That's ridicu — "

"She didn't take him seriously. She thought it was a big joke at first — and then — well, then it just made her mad. Then she wouldn't give him the *satisfaction* of being intimidated."

"But didn't Wynn know about it? Didn't *anyone*?"

"After it'd been going on for a while — that's when I found out about it. And then I told Greg."

"And couldn't you two do anything?"

"Hey, wait a minute!" For a split second Blake almost looked angry. "What could we do? No proof, no evidence — Dennis and I never got along, and *that* sure wasn't a secret — and Elizabeth had dumped the guy. Do you know how that would have sounded to the cops? They'd have called it high school soap opera. And if Greg had gone around telling tales about Dennis, he could have lost his job." He looked into Martha's shocked eyes. "Do you think I'm *proud* of myself for this? Hell, I can hardly stand to think about it." He jumped to his feet, hands in pockets and started pacing. "And Wynn . . . sure she knew about it . . . but if we'd made trouble for Dennis . . . well . . . he'd hinted to Elizabeth that he'd . . . make trouble . . . for Wynn."

Martha nodded woodenly, the implication clear. "Oh, Blake . . . I . . ."

"He killed her on Halloween." Blake looked across the deserted fields, his face sorrowful. "The last time I saw her, we were all at a party — she was making fun of Dennis — laughing about how immature he was — and then . . . well. . . ." He shook his head. "Later that night she left with him — and we never saw her alive again."

"Left with him! But — " Martha looked up at Blake, but he wasn't seeing her anymore.

"When we went to her house to look for her, Wynn found her — what was left of her — "

"Oh, no . . . stop. . . ."

"Up in her bedroom — "

"Which bedroom?" Martha murmured.

"What?"

"Which *bedroom*?"

"The one at the back of the house. Closest to the woods."

"Oh, God — "

"Wynn never got over it. She still has dreams — horrible nightmares. She still feels guilty because she let Elizabeth leave with Dennis and never told us — she was the first one in the house that night, and she still has times when she can't remember things — "

Martha's eyes were fixed on his face, his mouth, struggling to understand what he was saying, her mind as gray as the mist. . . .

"The next day they found Dennis's car in the river. It'd stormed all night and flooded, and the car'd been washed off the bridge. And they found the knife."

"So . . . they finally knew," Martha mumbled. She searched his face for some sign of satisfaction, but there was none.

"Murder-suicide they called it," Blake said hollowly. "But they never found him." He lowered dark eyes to her shocked face. "The current was just so strong . . . they never found Dennis."

Chapter 6

*You've got to be calm, Martha, you've got to be
grown-up about this and put it all in perspective
and not start jumping to conclusions. . . .*

Martha closed her eyes, thankful that another
exhausting day of school was over. There were so
many things she needed to know — but before she'd
been able to ask Blake about them, lunch break had
ended and he'd promised to call her tonight. Now
she glanced at Conor's hands on the steering wheel
and fought down a surge of anger.

"Oh, Dad," Martha muttered to herself, "why did
you ever get me into this?" She pressed her nose
flat against the window and stared out into black,
empty nothingness as the car sped home. In the
back bedroom closest to the woods . . . *her* bedroom. *No wonder I had that awful feeling . . . no
wonder. . . .* She hadn't been able to get it out of
her mind since her talk with Blake. Obscene phone
calls . . . pranks . . . a fire . . . Elizabeth's terror
in the last few seconds of her life. . . . It was all
so unbelievable, so terribly overwhelming, that

Martha could hardly stand to think about it. *And yet how can I not think about it, after all the things that have happened. . . .*

By the time they reached the house she still hadn't spoken a word to Conor, and he hadn't seemed the least bit bothered by her silence. While he tossed his books on the hall table and went about turning on lights, Martha sagged against the wall, facing the stairs like an old enemy. *I can't go up there right now, I just can't.* Conor disappeared into the kitchen, and a moment later she heard him whistling as he rattled pots and pans. Dragging her feet, she finally followed him and sank down at the table.

"I hope you cook better than your mom," she said.

The look Conor threw her was reproachful. "Everyone cooks better than my mom."

Martha hesitated, then announced, "I found out something today."

"So it would seem." Conor didn't even look up; now he was chopping onions on the cutting board.

"What's that supposed to mean?"

"It means I don't want to fight with you, even though you're sure in the mood for it."

Martha's mouth dropped open in surprise. For a moment she couldn't think of anything to say.

"Blake Chambers told you about Elizabeth Bedford's murder," Conor went on placidly. "Do you like your chili with or without beans?"

"I — " Martha stared at him, annoyed. "What were you doing spying on us?"

"You were the only two people sitting out there

on the bleachers in the rain in the middle of the football field. You weren't that hard to miss."

"Well then, how did you know what we were talking about?" Martha demanded. "How could you have known that?"

"In spite of what you think, I did happen to notice your wonderful mood on the way home." He wiped his knife on a paper towel and Martha shuddered. "And I did some detective work of my own."

"You did?"

"I cut class and went down to the newspaper office this morning. I read some pretty unpleasant stuff."

Martha sniffed. "Well, you don't know half of it, probably. Not all the really important details."

Conor gave a vague nod and started slicing cheese. "No, probably not."

She waited, but when he didn't say anything more, she gave a loud sigh. "All right, I guess I should tell you. Even though you sure weren't interested in anything on the way home."

This time Conor sighed. He put down the knife again, cleaned his hands on the dishrag, and turned and looked at her. "I figured you'd talk about it when you were ready. How much cheese do you want?"

Martha met his stare for a long moment, then grudgingly dropped her eyes. "I knew this was a horrible house from the very beginning. I knew it."

"Okay. Tell me all those really important details."

By the time Martha finished her story, the chili was simmering on the stove, but eating, for the time being, was forgotten. She repeated the story exactly as she'd heard it from Blake, and Conor sat across from her, elbows propped on the table, chin resting on hands, eyes lowered. His face showed no emotion — even when Martha recalled the grisly scene of the murder, Conor just listened, his face unmoved.

"Conor, are you in a trance or what? Have you even heard a single word I've said?" She waited expectantly, the silence lengthening between them. Something creaked in the hallway, and she glanced nervously towards the door. "Conor — "

"But they're not sure it was him," Conor said. "How can they be so sure it was him?"

"Of course it was him!" Martha stared, her calm snapping. "He was crazy and jealous, and he killed Elizabeth! In *my* bedroom! Conor, we shouldn't even be here — this house is bad luck — it's evil and dangerous! I don't want to live in a house that's supposed to be haunted — where someone was *killed*! Everybody talks about it! They all act like *I'm* weird and bad luck! I'll never have any friends. Nobody'll ever come out here to see us — "

Conor lifted his head slowly and looked at her. "You're talking like someone who believes in ghosts. I thought you didn't believe in ghosts."

"I — " her voice faltered. "All the . . . coincidences . . . the things happening around here — my room . . . the phone call . . . that scarecrow had a knife in him! — and that fire last night — "

"Oh. So now you don't believe I started it."

"This isn't funny!" Martha's hands clasped the

edge of the table. "Of course you started it — you *had* to have started it. Maybe the *house* made you start it — " She broke off, her eyes fixed on his, almost pleading. Her voice came out small and tight. "Well . . . *did* you?"

"No," Conor said. "I didn't."

"I don't believe you," Martha told him, and Conor rolled his eyes. "I don't know what to believe! I'm not staying in that room another night!"

"You don't have to," Conor said agreeably. "I'll change rooms with you if you want."

"Really?"

"Of course." He pulled himself up to his lean height and went over to the stove. "We'd better eat this stuff before it boils away."

"Oh, Conor, how can you even *think* about eating at a time like this?" Martha groaned. "This whole thing is just so awful — "

Conor regarded her a moment, then replaced the lid on the pot. "It's not awful. It's perfectly natural."

"Natural! Oh, right, it's natural that someone was murdered in the room where you're sleeping — it happens every day!"

"I'm not talking about the murder." Conor looked away, and Martha wondered if he was trying to hide a smile. "I'm talking about the house."

"And what could be natural about this horrible house?"

Conor remained unruffled. "When something so . . . so tragic happens in a house, it's natural that all those high-charged emotions should be . . . well . . . absorbed by it. By the rooms . . . the atmosphere. Sort of like . . . tangible memories."

"So what does that mean? It's the bad memories haunting our house?"

Conor stared at the stove, at the low blue flame sputtering on the burner. "It means . . . yes. Bad memories are haunting our house."

"Is that why my room is so cold?"

"Because it remembers, probably. Yes."

"So what about the fire last night?"

Conor hesitated. He averted his eyes, and Martha had the uneasy feeling that he was holding something back from her.

"It *could* have been an accident, right?" Martha insisted. "You *could* have just forgotten — left it on and gone to bed."

He gave a vague nod. "Maybe I had my mind on other things," he murmured.

"You *always* have your mind on other things. And you don't really believe what you just said, and you know it," Martha challenged him. "And next you're gonna tell me the phone call was just a joke, and the wind blew that scarecrow up in the tree, and my closet is just drafty, and there's absolutely *nothing* else in the house with us but bad memories — and — "

She shook her head in exasperation and hurried up to her room. For a long while she lay on her bed, her mind churning. *What was happening?* She was *terrified* being in this house — in this *room* — and maybe all those things really *were* coincidences, but Conor was holding something back, she could *feel* it — *but what?* And Dennis was dead, and *she* was in the room where he'd murdered Elizabeth in an insane rage. . . .

Something cracked against the windowpane.

Martha jumped up and switched off her light, edging cautiously towards the window. She could hear the wind wailing, a long mournful sound, and for one split second clouds struggled apart, splashing the ground with pale, pale moonlight. The trees arced back and forth in a slow kind of frenzy. Straining her eyes, Martha saw something on the ground below her window and realized a branch must have fallen and knocked against the house. She closed her eyes in relief, a headache beginning to pound behind her temples. *I should have eaten something . . . that was so stupid . . . I haven't really eaten anything all day. . . .*

The phone rang.

With a surge of relief Martha remembered that Blake was going to call, and she raced for the phone before Conor could answer it.

"Hello?"

"Hello, Elizabeth," the voice whispered.

And it wasn't Blake who drew a long, raspy breath . . . and let it out again . . . breathing . . . breathing . . . while her heart beat like a frantic wing in her throat.

"Who — who is this?"

It wasn't Blake who began to laugh and then suddenly went quiet — the awful, terrible silence going on and on forever. . . .

"Hello?" Martha cried. "Who *is* this!"

"You're dead, Elizabeth. Trick or treat."

Chapter 7

"Who was that?"

Martha spun around, the receiver clenched in her hand, and Conor pried it free. "I . . . he called me Elizabeth . . . he said I was dead. . . ."

"Dead, huh?" Conor considered this for a moment. "Nice touch. Wasn't I supposed to answer the phone from now on?"

"I thought — I mean, it was supposed to be for me," Martha stammered.

"Hmmm. . . ." Conor raised an eyebrow, but didn't pursue it. "Martha, don't say anything back to him. Don't even answer the phone, okay?"

"You didn't hear that breathing — he said 'Trick or treat' — just like before — "

"Martha, it's just a crank caller. Everyone in town knows that Elizabeth Bedford died here on Halloween — what did you expect him to say?"

"You still think this is funny, don't you?" Martha raged at him. "It's never entered your mind that something terrible might happen!" She ran to her room and slammed the door, bracing her body against it, trembling all over. *That voice! That horrible voice!*

"First there were the phone calls . . . he killed her on Halloween. . . ."

"No," Martha said sternly to herself, "it can't be happening again. Conor's right . . . someone's just trying to scare me."

"You're dead, Elizabeth."

She pressed her fists against her eyes, as if she could obliterate the blinding terror behind them. She hated Conor — *hated* him! So casual, like nothing had happened. Just preachy and patronizing and bossy and —

She jumped as the phone rang again. She heard Conor answer, then mumble, but she couldn't make out what he was saying. She put her ear to the door, then jumped again as he pounded on the other side.

"Martha, it's Blake," Conor said. "Do you think your heart can take this?"

Angrily she flung open the door and stomped past him, flashing him a look of loathing. Conor smiled and disappeared into his room, shutting his door behind him.

"Hello?"

"Hi. Hope I'm not interrupting anything important."

Martha shook her head, her palm already sweaty against the receiver. "No, I wasn't doing anything. I mean . . . just homework," she lied.

"Well, *that's* certainly not important," Blake chuckled. "Listen — Greg and Wynn are over here, and we thought we'd go out for pizza — it'd just be

73

for an hour or so — why don't you come along?"

"Me?" Martha couldn't believe her ears. "I mean — now?"

"Hey, it's okay if you've got something else going on — I know it's kind of short notice and — "

"No, I'd love to go. I'm starving."

Blake laughed. "Great. We'll pick you up in, say, half an hour. Oh, and Wynn says to come grubby — it's a real dump."

"I'll be ready," Martha promised. She hung up the phone in a daze, then scrambled to her room to look for something to wear. As she started downstairs, she noticed Conor's door slightly ajar and stood looking at it resentfully. She supposed she ought to tell him she was going out, but it irked her having to tell him anything. Finally she knocked and inched the door open.

He was sitting on his bed, papers spread out around him, a clipboard on his knees. At first she wasn't sure he'd even heard her, then he raised his head, one eyebrow lifting at the intrusion.

"I'm going out," Martha announced.

Conor nodded and went back to his papers. "Have fun."

Martha stood there, staring at his bent head, the thick mane of hair obscuring his features. "I don't know how long I'll be gone. It might be a long time."

"Okay," Conor said.

Martha started to say more, then clamped her lips together and closed the door. Then she opened it.

Conor didn't look up.

"I'm going out for pizza. With some friends."

"Lucky you."

Martha slammed the door and went downstairs to wait.

When Greg's car finally stopped in the drive, it was Blake who hopped out to help her into the back and then sat beside her. Wynn huddled next to Greg in the front, keeping her face turned from the house, but she gave Martha a nervous smile.

"Martha, my newest and prettiest student, how's life treating you at dear old Bedford?" Greg turned and winked at her, and Martha glanced over at Blake, feeling suddenly shy.

"Come on," Blake shot back. "She hasn't been here long enough to even *live* the Bedford life."

"Well, we'll fix that," Greg decided, steering the car onto the road. "We'll take you on the exclusive cruise — Bedford by night."

Wynn looked amused at that. "You guys stop it. Nothing's open in Bedford past nine o'clock."

"Not even the sidewalks. They close up at eight." Blake grinned at Martha. "We're going to the hot spot in town, though. *It* doesn't close till eleven tonight."

Martha leaned back, letting the banter rush over her in warm, soothing waves. It was so good to be with people again — people who weren't total strangers, hearing the laughter and jokes and good-hearted insults. The cousins shared an obvious camaraderie, and that cheered her like nothing had for a long time.

The pizza place was noisy and crowded. As Blake

led the way to a back booth, it was obvious to Martha that everyone knew everyone else, and they were *all* staring at her. *Is one of them the voice on the phone?* She bent her head and studied the menu, feeling a mixture of embarrassment and apprehension. She was glad when Greg finally ordered and they all started talking again.

"Have you written your ghost story yet?" Wynn asked. Blake and Greg were arguing loudly about the basketball coach, and she leaned across the table towards Martha.

"No," Martha said. "I really haven't thought about it." *It's the last thing I want to think about right now.* . . .

Wynn shook her head; she looked unhappy. "I wish the class had voted on something else."

"A romance?" Greg bent close to her, lowering his voice dramatically. "A mysterious stranger who sneaks into girls' rooms at night and — "

"A stranger with sexy blue eyes," added Blake as Wynn tried to push Greg away.

"Look at her, she blushes every time," Greg deadpanned. "Every time we mention that blue-eyed stranger — "

"It's true," Blake nodded. "He just has something the rest of us guys don't have — "

Wynn bent her face into her hands as they laughed. "You two — will you *please* — "

"We're a little upset with Wynn," Blake said seriously to Martha. "See, we *really* wanted to invite your brother but — "

"Blake!" Wynn's face went a deep scarlet, and

she looked so distressed that even Martha found it hard not to laugh.

"No, Wynn said we couldn't ask your brother," Greg continued, just as solemn. "She said she wouldn't come if *he* came, so — "

"It was between Wynn and the blue-eyed stranger," Blake said. "And I hated to see her starve, so — "

"Stop," Wynn moaned, but she was laughing now, in spite of their teasing. As it suddenly dawned on Martha that Conor was the topic of their conversation, she looked at Wynn in barely concealed astonishment.

"Conor? If *he* had come, I wouldn't have come, either. Then you'd have missed out on both of us." It was said before she even thought, but the guys burst into laughter, and Wynn cast her a grateful smile.

"Then we made the right decision." Blake shook Greg's hand, nodding emphatically. "After all, there's only room for two real men at this table."

"Then you'd better leave so they can sit down with us," Wynn threw back and looked smugly at Martha.

"So what's the story with your brother, anyway?" Blake asked Martha, draping his arm casually over the seat behind her. "Besides the fact that he's obviously a genius and has every girl in Bedford fantasizing."

"Stepbrother," Martha said automatically. "And I didn't know he *was* a genius."

"Are you kidding? I'm in three classes with him,

and he knows *everything*. The guy's a walking encyclopedia."

"You mean he actually talks in class?" Martha looked doubtful. "He hardly says a word at home."

"Well, let's put it this way." Blake spread his hands, explaining. "He never volunteers — *never* speaks up. But if he's called on — watch out. By the end of class, he and the teacher are in some deep discussion, and the class is hanging on every word. It's incredible."

"He must read a lot," Greg surmised, and Martha squirmed uncomfortably.

"I don't know."

"Maybe he's got one of those photographic memories," Blake suggested. "What does he do around the house?"

Martha cleared her throat, conscious of their eyes upon her. "I don't really know."

"You don't know? You live with him, don't you?" Blake laughed, but Wynn came to Martha's defense.

"She hasn't known him that long. They practically just met."

This time it was Martha who looked grateful. "He keeps to himself a lot. He's sort of in his own world."

"And to top it off, he plays a *mean* game of basketball." Blake shook his head in mild disbelief.

"He cooks," Martha added, and Blake rolled his eyes.

"Naturally."

"And he likes to walk in the woods."

"That's nice," Wynn said. "It's sensitive and — "

"And what?" Greg nudged her.

"Nothing."

"Come on, you were going to say 'romantic,' weren't you?" Blake picked up mischievously.

"Well, suppose I was." Wynn lifted her chin. "We could sure use some guys around here with a little sensitivity."

Blake and Greg groaned in unison, then cheered as the pizza arrived. For a while Conor was forgotten as they attacked their food and talked about other things: school, sports, the town. Martha laughed uproariously as Greg recalled childhood escapades that he and his cousins had been involved in, and then Wynn retaliated with some choice stories of her own that Blake and Greg swore had never happened. Martha couldn't remember when she'd had such fun, and she hated the evening to end.

After dropping Wynn off, Greg insisted that Blake borrow his car to drive Martha home. And though Martha felt shy about being alone with Blake, he soon put her at ease, driving around town as Greg had suggested earlier, showing her the general layout of Bedford. They took their time, talking, listening to tapes, and when the heater got temperamental, Blake's arm slipped easily around her shoulders and stayed there the rest of the way home. They drove slowly because of the fog, and Blake didn't seem in any hurry to drop her off — and when they finally pulled up in the driveway, Martha realized she hadn't thought about Conor or the house all evening. Conor's light was on, which seemed to amuse Blake. He helped her out of the car and took her hand, walking her to the porch.

"I'm glad you came," he said.

"Me, too." They looked at each other for a long moment, and he gathered her into his jacket, resting his chin on top of her head. His touch felt warm and secure.

"I've been thinking . . . being the official welcome committee definitely has its advantages."

"How's that?" Martha couldn't look away from his laughing eyes.

"I get first dibs on the new kid," Blake said in mock seriousness.

Martha laughed, embarrassed, then her voice grew urgent. "Do people here like to play jokes on the new kid?"

Blake looked puzzled. "Jokes? What kind of jokes?"

"Oh," Martha shrugged evasively, "stupid phone calls . . . things like that. . . ."

Blake studied her, his smile uncertain. "You mean Prince-Albert-in-a-can phone calls? It wouldn't surprise me — there're *lots* of dumb kids in Bedford." His smile widened as he pulled her closer. "Lucky Conor." Blake looked down at her, teasing, and Martha frowned.

"What's lucky about Conor?"

"He gets to live with you." Blake grinned again, his hand sliding from her arm. "I'll call you," he said. "See you tomorrow."

Martha stood there and watched as the car disappeared into the woods. Her heart felt almost sick with excitement, and her insides were still shaking.

Blake Chambers? With her? She was almost afraid to believe it was possible. A guy like that without a single serious girlfriend in the whole school? *There must be something wrong with him.* . . . And then she sighed and shook her head. *No, there's nothing wrong with him. He's absolutely perfect, he's the most perfect boy I've ever met in my life.* . . .

"Dreamer," Martha muttered to herself. "When you wake up, you'll be sorry." She turned the door-knob and groaned. It was locked. "Conor!" she called. She pounded and put her ear to the door to listen. No footsteps coming down the stairs. No answer from within. "Conor!" Martha called again. How stupid, going off without a key. Conor would never let her forget this one. "Conor! Come on, let me in! It's cold out here!"

Martha tucked her hands inside her jacket and stomped her feet. He'd probably fallen asleep study-ing, cramming his mind with all those genius things. She didn't know what Wynn saw in him, but she could tell Wynn was definitely interested and too shy to pursue it. *Maybe I'll help her out.* She really liked Wynn — maybe she'd introduce them in just the right environment and Conor would ask Wynn for a date, and then he'd turn into a normal person.

"Conor!" Irritated, Martha stepped off the porch and looked up at Conor's window. The light was still on, but there was no sign of movement. He probably had a headset on or something — she'd be out here screaming for hours before she heard her. Then an-other thought struck her — maybe he was in the bathroom — clear at the back of the house.

The wind was so cold, she was covered with goosebumps. On a hunch she tried the casements on the terrace at the side of the house, but all the rooms were locked. "Damn you, Conor." She kept close to the house and went on around, her eyes darting nervously at every sound, every shadow. She hadn't thought about the phone call till now — now it came back to her with frightening clarity — the voice — the breathing — *"you're dead . . . dead. . . ."*

A mournful cry floated from the trees, stopping Martha in her tracks. Only an owl, she told herself firmly — *keep moving. . . .* But the yard was alive with foggy shapes, and the house rose like a giant tomb against the night.

"Conor!" She was behind the house now, but there were no lights. The porch lay deep in blackness, and the wind was a muffled roar, carrying away her cries. She craned her neck, trying to pick out the bathroom window — the small one — there — right next to the window of her own empty room. . . .

Her own empty room. . . .

Except it wasn't empty.

As Martha's eyes widened in mute horror, she saw a pale light pass over the ceiling, throwing grotesque shadows on the walls. . . .

A pale light that flickered as it moved . . . then stopped . . . moved . . . stopped . . . as if it were lost. . . .

As if it were searching. . . .

"You're dead, Elizabeth . . . trick or treat. . . ."

And Martha's hand flew to her mouth, stifling her scream, as a silhouette slowly materialized out of those deep black shadows in her room. . . .

As a silhouette took shape in the window above . . . uncoiling and lengthening up the flickering wall. . . .

A person . . . suspended there. . . .

Watching her.

Chapter 8

"Conor!"

Martha beat her fists so hard against the front door that the whole porch shook. Almost at once a light came on and as Conor let her in, Martha fell on him, her eyes wild.

"Conor, there's someone in my room! Call the police! *Hurry!*" She hurtled past him, only to stop again, spinning around in horror. "What's the *matter* with you — someone's *up* there! I can't go by myself!"

Looking totally baffled, Conor went obediently up the stairs and straight to Martha's bedroom. As she huddled outside in the hall he turned on her light and checked the closet, then stood in the middle of her floor, looking around.

"There's nothing here."

"There *was* something here. *Someone* here. Conor, I saw them, I really — " She was still in the hallway, afraid to walk through the door, and Conor came out again, eyeing her curiously. "I didn't have my key, and you wouldn't let me in, so I went around to the back to see if you were in the bath-room, and there was this light in my room, and someone was at the window — " She crossed to the window then and looked out, searching the shadowy lawn below. "He *was* here — right here — looking out and — " She wheeled around and faced Conor, who was watching her in silence. "Why wouldn't you let me in?" she asked tightly.

His face was unreadable, not even a sign of denial. He just stood there, his deep blue eyes full on hers. After a long moment his shoulders stirred slightly. "Martha . . . maybe we'd better talk about this in the morning after — "

"After what? After you have another chance to scare me to death?" *The scarecrow . . . the graveyard . . . the fire. . . .* "Why are you *looking* at me like that!"

"Excuse me," said Conor. "I'll see you tomorrow when your sanity comes back."

Martha felt dangerously close to tears, but Conor's face hadn't changed. "You knew I didn't have a house key tonight and you figured I'd try the back door and you stood up here and watched me — "

"Watched you do what?" This time his mouth twitched, but not in amusement — more in a battle for patience.

Martha stepped away from him, her mind racing. *Could there be another phone line in the house that I don't even know about?* "I think — " Her mind faltered and went blank. *I don't even know what I'm thinking anymore, I'm not even thinking at all —*

"It could have been clouds breaking. It could have been me turning on the hall lights." Conor sighed. "It could have been lots of things. I'll sleep in here tonight. You take my room." When Martha shook her head he hesitated . . . shrugged. "Okay, then, Martha, do what you want."

She let him get to the other end of the hall before she finally spoke. "I changed my mind."

He didn't seem the least bit surprised. He waited while she grabbed her things, and then he held his door open for her, making a mock bow as she went inside. She slammed the door behind her and stood looking at his bed, his books scattered carelessly around, his shirt draped over the back of a chair. She felt so strange being here in his room . . . even stranger climbing into his bed. For a long, long while she lay there. And when she finally dreamed, she ran and ran through the black maze of the house, pursued by a shadow with no face.

Martha overslept the next morning and, going to school, she was so busy cramming for a test she'd forgotten about that she didn't have time for suspicions about Conor. She failed the test, but her spirits lifted a little when she saw Wynn waiting by her locker at lunch.

"You look tragic," Wynn said tactfully. "Wanna go for a walk?"

"I *feel* tragic. I'm working on flunking my junior year." Wynn looked properly sympathetic, and Martha went on. "What do you think of Conor? I mean, *really?*"

"I think I'd like him to carry me off and love me forever. Why? Is it that obvious?"

They stared at each other, then burst into laughter, heading outside into the cold.

"Oh, I'm just not good with boys," Wynn groaned.

"Don't be silly! When you walk down the halls they *all* say hello to you — they *all* knew you at that pizza place."

"They *know* me, but they never ask me out. I'd rather be a stranger and have a date once in a while."

Martha turned up her collar and kept pace beside her friend. "I *am* a stranger, and it hasn't done me a bit of good. Not that I'm looking," Martha added hastily. "And I'd *love* to introduce you to Conor, only — " She broke off, frowning. How could she share her suspicions about Conor when Blake had asked her not to mention the house to Wynn?

"Only I'm too nervous," Wynn said innocently. "Martha, you're sweet to offer, and who *wouldn't* want to know Conor better — " She dropped her eyes, then cast Martha a troubled look. "Number one, I don't want you to think you're my friend just because of Conor."

Martha looked surprised. "I don't. I never *thought* to think that."

Wynn nodded, relieved. "Good. Some girls would, though. But I'm not like that. Friends are . . . important to me."

An ache went through Martha's heart as Wynn turned her face away. For one moment she wrestled with the idea of admitting that she knew about Elizabeth Bedford, but luckily Wynn saved her.

"Martha, my best friend died last year. You might have heard about it, 'cause the town's full of stories. Except nobody really talks to *me* about it 'cause they don't want to upset me. Only I wish they *would* talk to me about it, 'cause the truth is — well . . . I don't remember."

Martha stopped, only half conscious that the wind was whipping her hair around her face. She pulled a strand from the corner of her mouth and thought how sad Wynn's eyes looked as she stared back at her.

"I don't," Wynn said again. "I wish I did, but I don't remember a lot." She started walking again, and Martha's legs moved mechanically, trying to keep up. "They sent me to doctors, you know . . . and one even hypnotized me. But I still can't remember much about that night. People say I found my friend Elizabeth and that . . . that someone had killed her. . . ." She tucked her arms around herself, and her face was plaintive, like a little girl. "But, Martha, I really can't remember. I remember . . . terrible . . . horrible fear. And the long dark."

Martha was interested. "What's that? The long dark?"

But Wynn gave an irritated shrug. "Just . . . dark. Darkness that went on and on forever."

Martha thought a moment, picturing the house, the dark shadows, the dark corners, the dark secrets. . . .

"You can't imagine how awful it is." Wynn drew

a shaky breath. "Trying so hard . . . but just . . . nothing comes."

They turned off the school grounds and headed up Main Street, past rows of old-fashioned shops. Wynn's face was still troubled, but as she glanced over at Martha again, a slow smile began to replace the pain.

"That's why I acted funny yesterday when we came to pick you up at your house. I just haven't been back there for such a long time. But I worried and worried about it — I . . . I didn't want you to think it was you or anything — "

Martha reached over and gave her a hug. "I didn't think that. And thanks for telling me." For a second Wynn looked like she might cry, and Martha added quickly, "We don't ever have to talk about it. You don't ever have to come."

But to her surprise Wynn shook her head. "No, that's just it. I *want* to talk about it. I *need* to. And I want to come to your house, too — I just . . . have to get up my nerve."

"Whenever you want, it's okay." *And then you can tell me if the house is really evil . . . or if Conor's trying to drive me out of my mind.* There were so many questions Martha was dying to ask, but instead she said, "I've never been to this part of town before."

Wynn seemed ready to change the subject. "It's the original downtown — take my word for it, nothing's any different than it was when we were kids. In fact, it's probably the same as it was a *hundred* years ago." Wynn gave her a glance that was almost apologetic. "I'll bet you feel so trapped here, after Chicago. I'll bet you had millions of things to do back there."

Martha thought a moment, smiling. "There were lots of places to go. Now that I'm gone, I wish I'd done more. But what do *you* do here? You know, for fun?"

"Well, you saw the pizza place — everyone either hangs out there or this other place called Marty's — it's right at the edge of town, and they have a band."

"Ooh, I love music — "

"You wouldn't like this. They're not very good, and they never learn any new songs. I mean, after they play the same old stuff three times in a row, it gets boring."

Martha laughed. "Okay, forget Marty's. What else?"

"Clubs at school. And school dances. Sports, naturally. And church." Wynn made a face. "It's really — *really* — the pits." She glanced towards a storefront window and suddenly pulled Martha over to the display. "Oh, look — don't you love that sweater?"

"It'd look great on you — go try it on." Martha tugged on her arm, but Wynn held back.

"No — I'd only get depressed."

"Depressed! Why?"

Wynn shook her head. "If you were as shapeless as me, you'd never ask that question."

"You? Look at me — I have — " Martha pinched at her own ribs — "lots of extra insulation."

"You do not! You have a great shape!"

"Lumpy — "

"All in the right places. Listen — I still remember a few years back — when everyone was getting measured in gym class? Afterwards I found out *my* chest and Blake's were the same!"

"You're kidding!" Martha couldn't help herself; she doubled over with laughter while Wynn looked on helplessly.

"Would I kid about something like that? I'll never get over it as long as I live."

They both started laughing then, harder than ever, and after several moments Wynn finally caught her breath.

"Oh, well . . . not that there's anyone around here to impress, anyway. You just can't get too excited about guys you've known since kindergarten. No mystique."

Martha straightened up slowly, holding her aching sides. "I guess I never thought about that — there were always new kids coming and going where I lived."

Wynn studied her with a smile that was almost shy. "I'll bet you had lots of boyfriends, didn't you?"

They were walking again, side by side, and Martha looked up at the gray sky, sudden memories making her frown.

"A couple. God, I was stupid, though."

"What do you mean?"

Martha cast Wynn a sidelong glance, kicking at some crumpled paper on the sidewalk. The wind caught it and it flew crazily through the air, snagging at last at the foot of a fire hydrant.

"There was this one guy who really liked me. And he was nice, too — and cute — and . . . well . . . my dad thought he was wonderful and was thrilled we were going out."

Wynn nodded as if she knew what was coming.

"But I liked this other guy more . . . he was so cool and so handsome" — Martha gave a guilty laugh — "and he was such a jerk."

Wynn stopped and turned so abruptly that Martha ran into her.

"That's what people said about Dennis, too." Her eyes were wide and serious. "That's just like Dennis and Elizabeth."

Startled, Martha watched Wynn walk away, then took a deep breath and hurried after her.

"Wynn!"

The girl stopped, shoulders rigid, hands clenched at her sides. As Martha slowed down, Wynn suddenly whirled to face her.

"They're wrong, you know. All of them."

Martha stared at her, mind racing. "About what?"

"About Dennis. Oh, he *could* be a real jerk sometimes, and he was always getting into some kind of trouble — and everyone thinks he killed Elizabeth — but he *didn't*. He couldn't have. He *loved* her." Wynn's face was almost pleading, and Martha reached out for her.

"I . . . Conor heard they broke up," she said. "That Dennis was kind of upset about it."

"Yes." Wynn was nodding, her eyes closed tight,

her voice suddenly sad. "Yes, that's true — they *did* break up and he wanted her back, but she didn't *want* to go back with him. He was jealous, that's all, just 'cause she was with somebody else and not him — but he *never* would have done something so awful — "

"Wait a minute," Martha interrupted. "After they broke up, she had a new boyfriend?"

"She went with Blake," Wynn said quietly. And then, seeing the look on Martha's face, "He never talks about it. He keeps everything in. And when you came and moved into her house — it really shook everyone up. Not just Blake and me, but . . . well . . . everybody."

Martha was staring at her, Wynn's words reaching her as from a long way off. "Wynn . . . what are you talking about?"

"She was small like you . . . and her hair was blonde. Even about the same length." Wynn's face was sad and apologetic, and Martha felt herself going cold. "Even the things you and I laugh about — and you're such a nice person, Martha. . . . You're just so much like her. You remind me so much of Elizabeth."

Chapter 9

That night it started to rain in earnest.

And Martha dreamed she was Elizabeth Bedford.

She'd drifted off restlessly, lulled by the dull thudding of rain against the windowpane, yet once sleep took over she lay there with the strangest sensation of wakefulness . . . as if part of herself were trapped inside her mind while the other part waited in the terror of reality.

She dreamed she was dying.

She felt each stab of the knife going through her, and everywhere she turned there were blood-spattered walls — and her killer was real, but she couldn't see his face because he was wearing a mask. . . .

Yet she knew him.

In her absolute terror she knew him, and knew she had trusted him with her life.

In the depths of her dream she screamed — screamed — and suddenly it was real; suddenly someone was holding her and she was safe at last in a pair of strong, steady arms.

"Martha, it's only a dream. You're okay."

And Conor was there, and his arms were around her, and the light spilling in from the hall was safe and real. . . .

"I'm dead," Martha whispered, and she began to cry, and Conor held her tighter and rocked her.

"No. It was only a nightmare. Go back to sleep."

"I'm scared," Martha said, but her voice was muffled against his bare shoulder, and sleep was a deep, deep sea, pulling her down.

"Then I'll stay," Conor said, far, far away, and she sank into stillness at last.

When morning came she felt drained and exhausted — she couldn't remember what had been a dream and what had been real, and she was embarrassed to go into the kitchen. Conor was at the table drinking coffee, scanning a newspaper. Martha slipped groggily into her chair.

"I'm never going to school again," she announced.

Conor lowered one corner of the paper, raised an eyebrow, disappeared behind the financial section once more.

"I'm not," she repeated sullenly. "I can't face anyone ever again."

"I thought we got all this straightened out yesterday. You've been facing them all this time, Martha. Nothing's different."

"It's different," she insisted. "I look like a dead girl."

"You just need sleep."

"Conor, this isn't funny! I *look* like Elizabeth Bedford — "

"That's not what you told me Wynn said — she didn't say you *look* like her, she said you *remind* her of — "

"No wonder everyone's been staring at me. No wonder I feel like such a freak."

"They're staring at you because you're new and you never talk to anyone."

"I live in her house, and I look like her, too!" Martha caught her breath sharply. "Did I have a nightmare last night?"

"Yes."

"Oh, no." Martha covered her face with her hands. So Conor *had* been there. She'd never be able to face him again.

"You can come out," Conor said. "I won't look at you if you don't want me to." He sounded like he was trying not to laugh, and Martha pointedly ignored him.

"I'm not staying in Elizabeth's room," she said.

"Then if we're going to switch permanently, I need to move my things."

"Don't you realize how serious this is? I feel . . . doomed."

Her voice dropped dramatically, and Conor laid the paper down.

"You're scaring yourself. You know that, don't you?"

Martha hesitated . . . gave a guilty nod. "But don't you think the coincidences are just too . . . too weird? Blake said Elizabeth was being . . . well

. . . harrassed and. . . ." She trailed off, frowning down at the untouched bowl of cornflakes Conor had had waiting for her.

"You're not Elizabeth," Conor said, not unkindly. "Your life isn't her life."

"No . . . hers is over." Martha glanced up at him, then shrugged. "There's so much I don't understand. Blake and Wynn both say Dennis was a jerk. But Wynn says he really loved Elizabeth and wouldn't have hurt her."

Conor toyed with his cup, the handle going back and forth between his fingers. "So how would Wynn know?"

"I was thinking about that," Martha said. "Wynn probably knew him better than most people 'cause she was Elizabeth's best friend, and best friends tell each other everything. Elizabeth probably told her lots about Dennis."

"And Blake probably spent just as much time with him at school. They had classes together, and they were teammates."

"Blake said Dennis was a dirty player."

"He was an ace player. They both were. Every article I came across when I checked out the newspapers that day couldn't say enough about the two of them. They were the top scorers. I wouldn't be surprised if they were top rivals, too."

Martha nodded glumly. "And then Elizabeth started going out with Blake after she and Dennis broke up."

"You didn't tell me *that* yesterday."

"I guess I forgot."

Conor glanced at her, the eyebrow lifting again. "Eat your cereal. I'll go fish out the car."

"Is it that bad?"

"Probably. It rained all night, and it hasn't stopped yet."

"Great," Martha mumbled, "it matches my mood."

The day dragged on relentlessly. Walking down the halls was pure torture — she was sure she could see fear and Elizabeth Bedford written in everyone's eyes. She had quizzes in three classes that she wasn't prepared for, and when Greg questioned her on a reading assignment, she realized she'd studied the wrong chapters. In between she managed to knock over a bottle of hand lotion in her locker, spotting most of her books with grease. When she realized there were papers due in her last two classes that she hadn't done, she leaned her head on her locker, feeling too hopeless to even cry, and never even noticed that Blake had come up beside her.

"Hi." He grinned. "You look like you could use a change of scene."

After the initial leap, Martha's heart settled sickeningly in her stomach. She thought of what Wynn had told her about Blake and Elizabeth Bedford, and she concentrated on rearranging her locker. *Well, it was nice while it lasted. . . .*

"What's the matter? Can't stand to tear yourself away from this place?" He slid his hand beneath her elbow and bent close to her ear. "I have to pick up some stuff for Wynn's decorating committee. Why don't you cut class and come with me?"

Martha felt shivers up her spine as his chin brushed the side of her face. "I can't just not go to class — I — "

Blake drew back, disappointed. "It'll be a chance to show you some of the scenery — come on, who's gonna know?"

"Oh . . . I . . . I don't know."

"Say you got sick."

"But Conor — he'll be waiting after school — "

"I'll get a message to him. One of the secretaries owes me a favor." He winked. "I'll have you safe at home by the time Conor gets there. Cross my heart."

Martha looked into his eyes, his persuasive grin. "Well. . . ."

"What do I have to do, beg?" Blake laughed then, and the last of her defenses crumbled.

"Okay."

"Great. Let me give the word to Terry, and I'll meet you by the gate. Five minutes."

It was still raining when she went outside — a steady stream turning the world to a gray, soggy mess. Martha had scarcely reached the gate when Blake was beside her, shielding her head with a notebook as he guided her to a van. Within minutes they were warm and cozy, and Martha settled back, allowing herself a luxurious sigh.

"Bad day?" Blake seemed genuinely concerned, and Martha gave a wry smile.

"Bad day? Bad week, bad month . . . bad life." She glanced away then, laughing to herself. "Sorry.

I'm not very good company." *I'm not like Eliza-beth. . . .*

"Hey — " Blake leaned over, his fingers on her arm, "would I have kidnapped you if I believed that?"

Martha half smiled. "Thanks for asking me to come."

"My pleasure." Blake inclined his head, then fastened his eyes back on the road. "We're going to Whitley — it's about twenty miles. You'll like it — nice old buildings, smaller than Bedford, so there's more countryside. My grandparents used to have a farm there, but they sold it to my cousins before they died."

"Do you ever go back there to see it?"

"Sure, that's where we're headed now. My mom goes every week to pick up vegetables they're always canning for us."

"Ummm. I wish Sally would learn about good food."

"Who's Sally?"

"Oh. Conor's mother."

"You like her?"

"She's okay. She's an artist, and she's kind of a slob most of the time. But I think her work must be pretty good — she's in galleries in New York and places like that."

"No kidding. You guys really *are* famous."

"Hardly." Martha looked out at the bleary trees and rain-beaten meadows. "My mother died two years ago," she said softly. "She wasn't at all like Sally."

Blake's eyes fell upon her face, his smile sad. "I'm really sorry, Martha."

"Oh" — she waved him away, a laugh catching in her throat — "don't be. Hey, I have a brand-new family now. Lucky me."

"You are lucky." His voice sounded so serious that she glanced up in surprise. "Conor seems like someone you can depend on — believe me, that means a lot." And before she could ask him what he meant, he broke into his carefree grin. "Hey, what'd I tell you? Smalltown, USA."

As the van began its descent into a narrow valley, Martha straightened in her seat to get a better view. A little village lay before them: roofs, chimney tops, and one white church spire all postcard-perfect through the veil of rain. Blake slowed to a crawl and began identifying things along the way — feedstore, market, post office, garage. Several old men in overalls, recognizing the car, gave lackadaisical waves, and Blake honked the horn in reply, swerving as a mangy dog took its time crossing in front of them.

"Feel like you're in a time warp?" Blake teased.

"Actually it feels very nice."

"Good, I don't want to bore you. Even if the decorating committee *is* counting on me."

"What are they decorating for?"

"The Halloween dance."

At Martha's questioning look, Blake struck his palm against his forehead in mock alarm. "What! At Bedford nearly a week and so uninformed!" He wagged an accusing finger at her. "*You* haven't been reading the posters in the halls."

Martha's mind raced. There *had* been something, she remembered now — some announcement about a dance, on big orange posters all over the school — but she hadn't really paid much attention to them. *Why should I? I won't be going.* . . . She glanced sheepishly at Blake. "I . . . sort of remember — "

"Ah ha. Well, it's Sunday night this year, and they're giving us Monday off. The party's an annual thing — probably the reason nobody thought to enlighten you."

Martha stared at him, something gelling in her memory. "A party . . . like the one last year?" *The last time you saw Elizabeth alive.* . . .

"Yes," Blake said quietly. He didn't look at her again until they were several more miles past town, and Martha felt the van slowing down. "This is it." Blake hopped out to unfasten a gate blocking a dirt road, and presently they pulled up in front of a farmhouse.

"Are you sure we should drop in like this?" Martha asked anxiously, but Blake was already opening her door.

"Oh, there's nobody home — they're in the city today. Come on." He took her hand and they ran across a muddy stretch of yard to a huge barn.

The warm, dusty interior felt wonderful after their dash through the rain. As Martha squeezed water from her hair, Blake pulled some blankets from a stall and tucked one around her shoulders, using one frayed corner to wipe raindrops from her cheek. Martha looked away, flustered.

"Hope you're not susceptible to pneumonia," Blake teased. "I'm drenched." He walked off a short distance and shrugged out of his jacket. "See up there?"

Martha looked where he pointed and saw a high, open loft heaped with mounds of hay.

"We used to have contests — Greg and I. We'd jump off and see who could land the farthest away."

"You could have killed yourselves."

"You're right," he chuckled. "And Wynn *always* told on us. Come on — " Before Martha could protest, he took her hand and started up the ladder.

"Blake — what are you — ?"

"Relax," he laughed. "I want you to see the view. I used to think I was on top of the world up here."

The blanket fell from her shoulders as she grasped the ladder and started up. As her head cleared the platform, she saw Blake wrestling with the doors, a fine spray of wind wetting his face as he stood looking out at the sodden landscape.

"Here" — he motioned her close and swept one arm out in front of him — "see that? There were even fewer houses over there when we were kids. You could see for miles and miles, and it was only fields."

Martha stood beside him, shivering in the piercing dampness. The town and valley lay at their feet — a checkerboard of dark green and rusty brown and gold, the hills muted, the bare woodlands swathed in gray.

"Cold?" In spite of her efforts to hide it, Blake

noticed her shaking and promptly shut the doors.

"Oh, don't do that — I — "

"No, it's cozier this way." He grinned and threw himself down on the hay, making a place beside him. "There's room for one more."

Martha hesitated, and Blake's smile widened. He lay back, head pillowed on his arms, and Martha gave in and sat down. Overhead the rain had settled to a gentle rhythm, and a sudden growl of thunder faded miles and miles away.

"Does it make you sad?" Martha stole a look at him. "Having things change. Thinking maybe someday you might have to leave this?"

"Are you kidding? I want to leave it. I can't wait to leave it."

Martha leaned back, regarding him in astonishment. "But I thought — you said — "

"I know, and sure, I love this place. But what kind of future would I have if I stuck around here?" His laugh was almost an afterthought. "I wouldn't stand a chance in hell of ever being anything."

Martha studied him a moment, the grim lines that had formed suddenly around his mouth, the flash of anger in his eyes. "What kind of anything?" she asked gently.

The hard look vanished, replaced almost immediately by a fierce gleam of hope. "Do you know how close I am to a basketball scholarship? So close I can taste it, Martha. I've got the reputation and the grades — and I hear it's a pretty sure thing." He paused, letting the words sink in. "A sure thing. . . ."

Martha looked down at her fingers clasped tightly in her lap. The silence was long before Blake spoke again.

"You think I'm selfish for wanting it so bad, don't you? But you don't know how it is here . . . how people are just *waiting* for you to fail and be stuck here like them for the rest of your life. God, I'd do *anything* to get away." He turned his head so that his eyes rested full on her face. They looked deep and sad. "Basketball's my ticket out of here, Martha. It's what I really *want*. What I really want to do. To *be*." She couldn't look away from that urgent stare, and suddenly his hand was on her arm, his fingers sliding up under her sleeve. "I . . . uh . . . don't usually go around making true confessions to everyone I meet." His laugh was embarrassed, but Martha gave him a reassuring smile.

"And I don't pass on true confessions, so you don't need to worry."

His hand tightened on her wrist. Slowly he drew her down so that their faces were only inches apart.

"You're really something," he said quietly, and there was only the soft patter of rain and the soft flutter of birds high in the rafters. . . .

And Blake's lips, soft . . . soft upon hers. . . .

"Don't," Martha murmured, and her hand pushed weakly against his chest, her eyes hurt and confused. "Why didn't you tell me I remind you of Elizabeth?"

Blake looked like he'd been struck. For an endless moment he gazed down at her, his eyes growing as hurt as her own. "Elizabeth?" He could hardly get the word out. "You? Remind me of her? Damn!" He didn't mean to push her away so roughly, but Martha sprawled back on her elbows. "Why in the hell would you ever think that?"

Martha rubbed her wrist where his fingers had left a mark. "Maybe we'd better just pick up those decorations and — "

"No. Not until we talk about this." Blake looked off, shaking his head slowly. "I admit, that first time I saw you in the store, you sorta looked like her from the back. . . ." He glanced at her reprovingly. "But it never went any farther than that."

Martha was acutely aware of his closeness now . . . his fingers beneath her chin, tilting her head so he could look at her.

"I liked you the first time I saw you, Martha. You were so honest and open . . . so cute . . . and I felt like I really wanted to get to know you better."

Martha felt the color rise in her cheeks at his intense scrutiny. "You . . . you never told me you were serious about her."

His head moved slightly. "We were close for a while. That's all. It didn't seem important enough to tell you. And anyway, it's in the past. It has nothing to do with you and me . . . now."

His lips closed over hers. Martha caught her breath as his body pressed her gently down in the hay. He was so strong, yet so tender . . . and after an endless kiss, he looked down at her and smiled.

"I guess I'd better get you back. I don't want your brother calling out the troops."

"Stepbrother," Martha murmured. "And he

won't even know I'm gone." The last thing she wanted to think about right now was Conor and the house . . . the last thing she ever wanted to do was leave this warm, blissful haven and Blake's arms.

Blake glanced at his watch and groaned. "Just my luck, he probably has a black belt in karate — the *one* thing I can't do."

Martha came slowly back to reality. Blake's body still pinned her lazily to the floor, and she could still feel his kiss upon her lips. "If I had to guess," she said breathlessly, "I'd say Conor's a total pacifist."

"If you had to guess?" Blake teased. "You mean you still don't know anything about him?"

Martha shrugged, impatient to change the bothersome topic. "Don't you have some decorations to pick up?"

"Is *that* what I came for?" Blake asked innocently, then gave her a slow grin. "And you're getting kind of bossy, aren't you? Ordering me around?"

"No — I only meant — " Martha squealed as Blake began tickling her, and as he finally gave in to her pleadings, he hopped up with a laugh, pulling her to her feet.

"The stuff's probably out in the shed, but I didn't bring you along to work, you know. Why don't you wait in the van? It'll be warmer."

Martha gave him a push, but he righted himself easily, looking pleased with himself. "Maybe I will. You deserve to slave out there all by yourself."

But work went faster with two, and after Blake pulled the van up to the shed, they lugged bales of straw, bundles of cornstalks, and dozens of pumpkins and tossed them into the back. By the time they were finally finished, Martha thought her arms would fall off.

Darkness was sifting down as they wound their way back towards the village. Martha leaned against the window, not really paying attention to the scenery, until something in a nearby field caught her eye. She hadn't noticed the little cemetery on their way to the farm; now in the gathering dusk it looked almost like a mirage.

"Has that cemetery been here a long time?" she asked, straightening to see out the window.

Blake followed the point of her finger and nodded. "It's used for both towns. Whitley was originally part of the Bedford estate till the family had to start parceling off the land. Everyone's buried here now — even the family."

"Then what about the one behind our house?" Martha asked. "I thought the Bedfords were all there."

"That's the *old* family and their servants. We're talking eighteen hundreds. The town talked about moving them here, but that old family crypt is kind of intimidating to a lot of people. They finally decided to let the old Bedfords rest in peace."

"So. . . ." Martha hesitated, not wanting to bring up the past again, but somehow, needing to know. "So . . . Elizabeth — "

"Yes, she's buried here." Blake's expression was very controlled. He glanced again at the cemetery in his rearview mirrow. "Dennis, too."

"Dennis? But I thought — "

"They put up a marker for him," Blake said scornfully. "In his memory. As if anyone would want to remember him. . . ."

For several miles they rode in silence. Martha chanced a look at Blake's face, and it was stony and strangely cold. When he mumbled something under his breath, it was so quiet that at first she didn't even hear him.

"They want him to be dead," he said again, and Martha looked over with a start. "Everybody wants him to be dead. Including me." Blake's hands tightened on the wheel, and when he looked back at her, his eyes were dark with an emotion Martha couldn't read.

"But . . . he *is* dead," she whispered.

And Blake shook his head, his voice suddenly sad. "But they never found him, Martha. What . . . what if — *somewhere* — Dennis is still alive?"

Chapter 10

"Well, we made it." Blake grinned triumphantly. "I think we beat him home."

Martha sat stiffly against the door, her stomach so knotted that it hurt. Ahead of her the house lay in silent shadows — it was full twilight, and they'd forgotten to leave a light on.

"Hey," Blake leaned over, peering anxiously into her face, "you're not upset over what I said back there, are you? I should never have — "

"Don't be silly. I'm not upset."

"Don't *you* be silly. You haven't said two words all the way home."

"I'm . . ." Martha thought quickly, "maybe I really *am* coming down with something."

"You can't." Blake grinned again, tilting her chin up with his finger. "You have to go to the Halloween party."

Martha stared at him, nothing registering. "Of course I'm not going to the Halloween party, I don't have a date — " She broke off, flustered, as he laughed.

"You do now. So hurry on inside and play sick for Conor and I'll see you later, okay?"

Martha's head was spinning. Somehow she told him good-bye and let herself into the house.

She didn't know why she hadn't asked him to stay.

Now, watching miserably as the van disappeared from sight, she wished she'd thought of some excuse to ask him in, to have him stay with her, just until Conor got home. . . .

Where is Conor anyway?

Martha pressed her hands to her temples, trying to squeeze away the doubts. *Never found . . . never.* She leaned back against the wall and slowly opened her eyes. Silence echoed around her — one gloomy staircase rose beside her, the upstairs swathed in shadows. She took a deep, shaky breath and pushed herself forward. *Damn you, Conor. . . .*

The lights. If she could just get all the lights turned on, that would help. If she could just stop thinking about what Blake had said and get all the lights turned on, then she'd be okay, and Conor would get home, and everything would be nice and normal. . . .

She found a switch, and the hallway stretched ahead of her like a dim tunnel. She saw the heavy draperies at the opposite end. . . .

The slight stir of velvet. . . .

The one fold, strangely out of line with the rest.

Her heart raced with terror. She wiped her sweaty palms on her skirt and backed away. *There are no such things as ghosts . . . there are no such things as evil houses. . . .*

She hurried up to her room, purposely averting her eyes from the yawning doorways as she passed. She shut the door, strangely uncomforted by the sight of her unmade bed, her books and records and posters, her dirty clothes on the floor in front of the closet. . . .

Martha's eyes fastened 'on the closet door, and she gave an involuntary shiver. How many ordinary, everyday things had suddenly become frightening to her since moving into this awful house? She *knew* better than to believe all the talk about this house, and yet how could she explain away the scary things that had happened to her here? Hadn't Conor said that a house could harbor bad memories — and where *was* Conor, anyway? What could possibly be keeping him so long?

They never found him. . . . What if Dennis is still alive?

Martha pulled her sweats from a drawer and banged it shut. She didn't want to think about Dennis now . . . not Dennis or Elizabeth Bedford or the Bedford house or the Bedford cemetery or — she'd just start getting her things together, like Conor had said, and move all her stuff into the other room — this would be a perfect time to do it and —

What was that?

Martha froze, her sweatshirt half over her head. As her eyes darted frantically from dresser to closet to bedroom door, she knew it wasn't just the chill that had caused her skin to break out in goosebumps. Something had floated up the stairs just then . . . along the hall to her room . . . a soft sound. . . .

A whispering sound.

Like invisible leaves blown across the wooden floor by a cold, invisible wind. . . .

"Conor?" Martha called.

The noise stopped.

Slowly she tiptoed to the door and put her ear against it, straining to hear over the pounding of her heart.

"Conor?" she called again, more softly this time. She inched the door open and peered out into the hallway. It was hazy with shadows, but she could see Conor's room from here, and it was still dark. *Besides, I would have heard the front door open . . . he would have said something.* . . . Unsettled, Martha eased the door back into place and wished it had a lock.

He *couldn't* be much longer — any minute she'd hear the car pull in and he'd walk into the house, weird as ever, and for the hundredth time she'd hear the rationalizations about old houses settling and drafts seeping in and. . . .

They never found him. . . .

Martha slammed a record on her stereo and turned it up. It was a love song, one of her favorites, and she curled up with the pillows on her bed and concentrated on trying to relax. Conor would be here any second now, and all the doors and windows were locked, and as long as the music played, the house couldn't trick her with old, scary sounds. . . . *I'll think of something nice . . . something wonderful.* She closed her eyes and thought of Blake so warm and strong beside her, and his lips so insistent on hers. . . . She turned her head dreamily as rain thrashed the windowpane, and then the music . . . and Blake . . . pulled her gently . . . gently . . . into a deep, dreamy embrace. . . .

She didn't know how long she'd dozed off, but she knew on some level of consciousness that something was wrong.

Fighting her way back from sleep she realized she'd just had another nightmare — where eyes watched her from unfathomable darkness — so close, so *near* to her, seeing every single thing she did . . . everything she even thought —

And then it was more than the eyes.

It was a presence.

A presence even stronger, even more frightening than the eyes had been — a presence so malevolent that it almost wasn't human. . . .

Martha's eyes flew open. For a long terrifying moment she lay there, bewildered and afraid, trying to figure out what was so *wrong* about the room —

And then she knew.

Her light was out.

The record, long since ended, scratched softly over and over again on the turntable. Rain hissed and streamed against the windowpane. As Martha's eyes painstakingly adjusted to the darkness, she turned her head slowly to her closet.

It was open.

And someone was standing inside.

The shriek that formed in her throat stuck there, threatening to choke her.

She could see the thing — only ten feet away from her bed — the dark, indistinct outline of someone standing there, not moving, not making a sound — just watching her with a terrible, silent patience.

A sliver of lightning flashed at the window. . . .

She saw the cold glint of his eyes.

He doesn't know I'm awake — and Martha's chest heaved as she fought to control her breathing — *dear God, he doesn't know I've seen him — he doesn't realize —*

A boom of thunder shook the house, rattling the very foundations.

The whole room — darkness — closet — tilted and swayed —

As Martha bolted up, she could see the whole closet now — how the shadows had shifted within and lost some of their blackness and terror —

The closet was empty.

And even as she snapped on the lamp, even as the room burst into soft colors and familiarity, even as she flung open the closet, filling it with light, she knew with dreadful certainty that she wouldn't find anything, nothing but the memory of a waking nightmare and the few clothes she ripped aside and flung back —

And when the phone rang, she was beside herself with fear and anger, and she raced into the hallway, furious that everyone had abandoned her, snatching up the receiver with uncontrollable panic —

"Conor! Where *are* you? You've got to come home — "

But he wasn't answering — he wasn't saying anything — just struggling to breathe — and then giving a soft laugh that chilled her heart —

"Elizabeth," the voice scolded, "don't you like being in the house all by yourself?"

"Who is this!" Martha screamed.

"You're mine, Elizabeth . . . trick or treat."

Chapter 11

As Martha raced to the front door, her hand made a grab for the doorknob — only to recoil again instantly.

The handle was turning.

She staggered back, eyes glued in horrible fascination on the handle moving . . . the door opening. . . .

Conor stood there, one hand still on the door, twisting the key from the lock. Martha sagged back against the wall and felt her knees give out, her body sliding slowly down until she was sitting on the floor looking up at him.

"Conor. . . ." She was struggling for control, struggling to breathe, struggling with every ounce of willpower not to scream hysterically. "Where the hell *were* you?"

"I had car trouble." For a long moment he surveyed her, in a crumpled heap, then he seemed to remember the rain and wind whooshing through the hall and closed the door. "Why?"

She couldn't speak. For several seconds her voice

seemed permanently displaced, and she could only look at him with dull eyes. Conor squatted down on his heels beside her.

"The phone," Martha said. It was even too much of an effort to explain, although Conor — for once — was giving her his undivided attention. She gazed back into his blue stare.

"He knew you weren't here. He knew I was alone." When Conor didn't respond, her voice grew frantic. "I think he was in my closet! *Again!* Doesn't anybody care what's *happening* around here!" Whirling to the stairs she ran smack into the newel post and grabbed her midsection with a groan.

Conor bent over her, easing her down onto the bottom step. "Your exit could use some work — are you okay?"

"Just leave me alone — you — " All her wind had been knocked out, and she could barely speak.

"All this," Conor sighed, "and the flu, too."

"What flu?" Martha moaned.

Conor sat beside her, half smiling. "The flu they told me you had at school. So how'd you get home? As if I couldn't guess."

Martha shot him a venomous look. "For your information, Blake just *happened* to come by when I started feeling bad, and he was *nice* enough to bring me home — "

"That was certainly lucky." Conor reached over and carefully pulled something from her hair as Martha tried to swat his hand away.

"At least he cares how I feel — " She stared down at the strands of hay Conor held between his fingers, and a rush of fire went through her cheeks.

"But I'm sure you feel much better now," Conor said diplomatically.

Somehow Martha made it up the stairs to the bedroom. *How she hated him — what had she ever done to deserve this stupid life she had now?* She felt like a caged animal, pacing round and round the room, snatching up her personal belongings, flinging her clothes from the closet until she'd inspected each hidden corner. *Something had been there! No, not something — someone!* It was a *person's* shape she'd seen hulking there in the shadows — *a human figure* — and she didn't care *who* wouldn't believe her, she *knew* what she'd seen.

She threw herself on the bed and screamed into the pillows, and after several good, long, muffled shrieks she rolled over and calmly decided she was having a nervous breakdown.

He must be out there watching . . . he had to be or how could he know? Slowly Martha went to the window. What had Blake said about Dennis — *"he'd tell her things he'd seen her do — like he'd been watching the house. . . ."* And where had Dennis hidden, Martha wondered now . . . out there in the woods . . . behind any one of those hundreds of trees . . . in the graveyard. . . .

They never found him.

Is he still out there even now . . . just like he was the other night in the woods . . . watching me? . . . "Oh, God." Martha drew a sharp breath and caught her head between her hands. She couldn't think about it — she didn't *dare* — *because as long as I don't believe in things, then they can't be real, they can't come true, they can't hurt me. . . .*

Frantically Martha jerked the blanket off the bed and rummaged in her desk for something to hang it with — tacks, pushpins, staples, nails — but there was nothing strong enough for a makeshift curtain. Conor had said nobody could see in, but Conor had been wrong because *somebody* — some horrible, breathing voice — was out there, knowing how terrified she was —

Martha froze.

Behind her the lamp quivered and the light skittered nervously along the ceiling.

This time she *knew* she hadn't imagined it.

The soft creaking sound. . . .

The soft stalking sound. . . .

Very close to her. . . .

Trying not to be heard.

Her whole body went numb.

She heard the squeak of hinges . . . the slide of wood against the floor . . . and still — *still* — she couldn't turn her head — couldn't force herself to look in the closet —

From the corner of her eye she watched the door move.

She saw the feet step noiselessly out of the dark —

And only then could she whirl and face the eyes that stared back at her from deep, black shadows.

Chapter 12

"Conor!" With a shriek Martha fell on him, all her rage and fear pouring out as she pummeled him with her fists and forced him back against the wall. Conor calmly dodged her blows, then with one expert twist, caught both her hands in his.

"Do you know," Conor said, "that there's a secret passageway from the butler's pantry straight here to your closet?"

Martha promptly kicked his shin. "I *hate* you, Conor! Do you *hear* me? I hate and detest and *despise* you!"

Conor's look was reproachful. "Oh, come on, don't gloss it over — tell me how you *really* feel!" He doubled over as a book sailed into his stomach, and just managed to duck the three notebooks that followed in quick succession. "Don't you at least want to explore it?"

"Get *out* of here — *get out!*" Martha was positively livid and as she lunged for her radio, her shoulders were suddenly caught and flattened upon the bed. "Get *off* of me!" she screamed.

Conor shook his head. "Now, Martha, someone's going to get hurt — and it's liable to be me." Her mouth opened but he put a finger to his lips. "Uh-uh . . . believe me, I *know* you hate me, detest me, *and* despise me, but I think it's time you and I had a serious talk about what's going on here."

Martha gave him her most poisonous look. "I think it's obvious what's going on here — *you've* been sneaking into my room, making sick phone calls, hiding in the woods, trying to scare the *life* out of me — some *joke*, Conor!"

"I don't know about this joke," Conor said. "I *do* know you're accusing me of some pretty strange things — "

"Conor — you're a pretty strange person."

"You don't even know me. You don't know anything about me."

His tone was so serious that the retort Martha was about to make died on her lips. He was bent over her, tawny hair framing his face, the light glowing around his head like a benevolent aura. His eyes were pure, blue pools, and with an effort she pulled her own eyes away.

"I know as much about you as you do about me," she muttered defensively.

Conor raised his chin, thinking, but his eyes never left her face. It was useless trying to free herself — he was holding her without any effort at all.

"You like Emily Dickinson and rock music, Mexican food, and you love to bake — brownies, mostly. Daisies are your favorite flowers, red's your favorite color, and you don't go much for white. You had lots of friends in Chicago — especially some guy named Ken — you love to write, and you're good at it, but you have absolutely no confidence in yourself. You had a cat you grew up with, you love animals, you feel like nobody takes you seriously, that they never listen, that they think you have an overactive imagination — "

For one horrible minute Martha thought she was going to cry. "They *do* think that!" she blurted out.

"Wrong," Conor said. "*I* don't think that."

She couldn't seem to break from his stare — then finally she turned her head and felt his hold on her relax.

"No more hysterics?" Conor asked. Martha shook her head, but his expression was still guarded.

"No more. I promise."

He nodded then and slid away from her, positioning himself on the edge of her bed. Martha lay there a moment longer, regarding him soberly.

"You didn't come into my room before? Into the closet? Or watch from the window? You swear?"

Conor signed a cross over his heart.

"The scarecrow," Martha said. "That was first." She waited for him to rationalize, but when he didn't, she went on hesitantly. "And then one night when I was outside by myself, I thought I heard someone crying — and I thought someone was there — "

"Where? Doing what?"

"I don't know . . . in the woods. Hiding. Watching me." He nodded encouragement and she sat up. "It was just a feeling — only more than a feeling — I was almost so sure it was real, I was terrified."

"Why didn't you say anything?"

"I was going to," Martha said quietly, "only . . . well . . . Dad's call came that night about Hawaii and . . ."

The all-too-familiar look crept across Conor's face, and he cast her a sidelong glance. "I get the gist."

"Well" — shamefaced, Martha hurried on — "then that one night I thought I saw the door move — that same night you smelled smoke — "

"I remember. You were staring at something when I came in your room."

"And then the other night when you fell asleep and I forgot my key — I was going around to the back of the house, and someone was up here — here in my room. I could see a shadow on the wall, going back and forth — and then he stood at the window."

"But you couldn't tell anything specific about him?"

Martha shook her head. "No — the light was sort of flickering, the way a candle does, and the shadow was all distorted. And then," she took a deep breath, "then tonight I fell asleep and when I woke up, the lamp was out — and it's happened before — don't look at me like that, Conor, I *didn't* turn it off — it was *on* when I dozed off — "

Conor's lips moved in a slow smile. "Maybe thirteen."

Martha looked at him blankly. "Maybe thirteen what?"

"Maybe you look thirteen instead of twelve when you're really passionate about something. Do you get passionate very often?"

"Conor — "

He held up both hands, the smile fading. "I just can't decide what's more fascinating — living in an evil house or having a sister."

"You're not listening to a thing I've said!"

"On the contrary, I've heard each word and locked it away in my mind. So when you woke up — "

Martha frowned at him, slowly relenting. "So when I woke up, there was something in my closet — no, *someone* — Conor, I could just make out the shape, and it was definitely human and it was definitely there." She huddled back against the pillows and pulled her knees up to her chin. "Do you . . . do *you* believe in dead people coming back to the scenes of their tragedies?"

For a long while there was only the brush of wind against the pane, the soft murmur of a sleepy rain. Conor looked down at the rug beside the bed and stretched out his legs.

"Yes, I believe that can happen."

Martha didn't know whether to be surprised or not — part of her wanted to shake him, to make him tell her that ghosts didn't really exist, that she was being silly, that —

"They never found Dennis," she reminded him.

Was it her imagination, or did Conor look uncomfortable? "And what if I really *do* look like Elizabeth," she added unhappily, "even if it *is* just from the back?"

"You don't look like Elizabeth," Conor said quietly, and her head came up.

"How would you know?"

"That day I went to the newspaper office, I saw her picture. You both have blonde hair. So what? *Lots* of people have blonde hair."

Martha stared at him.

"It's just that . . . well . . . you know . . . Blake went *out* with her."

"I'm sure Blake's gone out with every girl in Bedford."

Martha felt her heart splintering, but she managed to keep her voice under control. "Why are you even talking about Blake, anyway?"

"*You* were talking about Blake."

"Well, I don't want to talk about him anymore, okay? He . . . he's been very nice to me . . . he's really very, very sweet. . . ." She glanced over, ready to defend him, but Conor just stared back, his face infuriatingly neutral. "Anyway, you're just jealous," Martha muttered.

"Why should I be jealous? *I* don't want to go out with him."

"Can we please just talk about something else?" Martha's voice tightened; she could almost swear that there was a smile right behind Conor's eyes. "Dennis might be alive, and I look like Elizabeth, and Halloween's in three more days. Elizabeth was getting phone calls — I'm getting phone calls. She was being watched — and so am I. And there's a feeling in this house that won't go away — and I *know* I'm not imagining it."

"You're not," Conor said softly. "I feel it, too."

Martha's reply stuck in her throat as she stared at him. "You do? Wait a minute — you — "

"I felt it the first time I came inside — especially in this room." Conor's eyes swept the walls, the ceiling, the windowpane. "It's more than bad memories . . . something else. Like bad secrets."

Martha just gaped at him. "*You* felt the coldness in here?"

"Yes. This room's always been the worst."

"And you let *me* stay in it?"

"I didn't know you'd be so receptive." Conor had the grace to look a little sheepish. "Not many people are, you know."

"Then . . . you've *believed* me all this time?" Martha felt numb as anger and relief flooded through her.

"I never said I didn't believe you," Conor said quietly. "I never said that."

"No, you just let me believe I was imagining everything." Martha closed her eyes and buried her face in her hands. She was too numb even to scream at him. "Oh, Conor, how could you?"

"You were just so upset about everything." Conor went to the window and stood there, arms folded across his chest, staring out into the night. "It's been so much harder for you than me — having your whole world pulled out from under you. I just

". . . didn't want to make it any scarier."

In the long quiet, Martha thought he might have sighed, a weary sound like the rain coursing slowly down the window glass. She watched his shoulders, the easy grace of his body as he slowly leaned against the wall.

"It's been hard for you, too?" she asked in a small voice.

He gave a vague nod.

"I'm sorry," Martha said. "I didn't know. I didn't even dream — " She fumbled for words, but he looked up again, his face solemn.

"This house — " He waved his hands in an inclusive gesture. "I can't get rid of the feeling. It's . . . oppressive. Not like anything I've ever experienced before."

"What do you mean?" Martha huddled in the corner, pulling the blanket up over her feet, almost afraid for him to answer.

"The fire," Conor said.

"There was a fire when Elizabeth was here, too."

He nodded. "Martha, I did *not* start that fire." In one fluid movement he pushed himself from the wall and began pacing.

"You're absolutely sure?"

"Absolutely positive. I remember turning off the stove and even checking it again to make sure everything was off. I remember hanging the dish towel on the rack behind the door."

Martha ran her hands over her arms, already feeling the gooseflesh.

"And I *know* I didn't close the kitchen door."

He paused beside the bed, frowning down at her. "And then there's the cemetery." When she only looked back at him apprehensively, he added, "Martha . . . I think I was led there."

"What!"

"I know it sounds crazy, but one minute I was down in the study reading, and the next minute I was going into the woods."

Martha's lips moved soundlessly. When her question finally came it was scarcely more than a croak. "What led you? A voice or something?"

"Not a voice. But something, yes." He pondered a moment, moved his hands towards his heart. "Stronger even than a feeling. An insistence. An overpowering insistence."

"Like you were in a trance or hypnotized or something like that?"

The shake of his head was firm. "No, I was fully aware of what I was doing — I just couldn't ignore it, that's all. I couldn't *not* go."

Her mind raced back — back to that night in the graveyard and Conor's strange behavior at the — "Mausoleum," she murmured. "Something about the mausoleum — that's what had you so upset, wasn't it?"

His eyes settled on hers, deep and troubled. "There was such . . . danger. Such a sense of — " the look he flashed her was almost apologetic — "finality."

Martha's laugh was strained. "Conor — it was a *tomb* in a *cemetery*. You can't get much more final than that."

"No, it was more than that. I felt . . . like we were being threatened, somehow."

This time Martha didn't laugh. A fierce chill snaked through her body, and she hugged a pillow to her chest. She stared at him, and he stared back. "Conor," she whispered, "what's happening? What are we gonna do?"

"That fire didn't start by itself," Conor said slowly. "And something had to make that shadow on your bedroom window. . . ."

"You *do* believe me — " Martha's words stuck in her throat with a metallic taste of fear. "You really do — "

"There could be other hiding places in this old house." Conor's eyes strayed to the closet and stayed there.

Martha's own eyes grew wide as realization began to dawn. . . .

"Maybe this house really *is* haunted, Martha. But not by the kind of ghosts people think."

And as he stared out into the stormy night, unspoken possibilities hung between them like a cold, inescapable prophecy.

Chapter 13

"Martha?"

Martha nearly ricocheted off her locker as a hand came down on her arm. When she looked up, it was to find Greg Chambers looking down, a friendly but professional look on his face.

"Little jumpy, aren't you? Late night?"

Martha forced a grim smile and shrugged. She'd taken over Conor's room again last night, even though he'd boarded up the panel in her closet, but she hadn't slept — not with Conor's speculations pounding in her head and every nighttime noise a fatal danger.

"Why don't you step into my office?" Greg said amicably.

Martha stalled. "I . . . I have this history quiz — "

"I'll write you a note." He took her arm and steered her down the hall, shutting his office door, indicating the chair with a nod of his head. "With your test grades lately, one more bad one shouldn't matter too much, should it?" He slid behind his desk with a sly grin and leaned towards her. "Come on now, Martha, I'm not the enemy here, so let's have it, huh?"

Martha squirmed miserably in her seat and said, "Well . . . I've been kind of tired — "

"Tired!" He slapped his palm on a pile of papers, scattering them. "You look like a zombie. When was the last time you slept? Or ate, for that matter? If Blake's really serious about this, he'd better start taking better care of you." He chuckled as Martha blushed. "So — are you going to tell me the problem, or do I have to use all the clever little ploys I learned about in advisor school?"

"I'm just . . . not adjusting very well, I guess."

Greg nodded, fingers drumming on the desktop. "Your teachers are concerned — no, now, wait a minute — *concerned*, Martha, not out to get you. The transcripts you brought with you show a whole different kind of student. So how come *she* stayed back in Chicago?"

"She liked it there."

"Aah. Has she thought of coming for a little visit? Impressing us with her exceptional abilities?" His smile, so like Blake's, was irresistible, and Martha felt herself returning it. "That's better. What's wrong, Martha?"

Her smile melted, swallowed by a sick feeling inside. "It's . . . it's just the house. . . ."

"The house." Greg looked down at her file, running his thumb along the tab. "This . . . uh . . . wouldn't have anything to do with its history, would it?"

Martha shrugged noncommittally. The last thing in the world she wanted to talk about now was the house and all the terrors it opened up. She kept her eyes on his hands — lean and strong like Blake's. . . .

"Okay now, look." Greg sighed and fell back in his chair, swiveling a little as he snapped a rubber band. "Every town has its spooky old house and its eccentric old neighbors and its ridiculous old fairy tales. Bedford's no exception."

"It's no fairy tale. It really happened. Somebody was murdered."

"Okay. Somebody was murdered, and the murderer drowned. End of case. Every old house in the world probably has a death or two to its credit — natural or unnatural, as the case may be. So what's really bothering you? It can't be just haunted house gossip — "

Martha didn't want to go into it. Here in the warm confines of Greg's office all the terrors seemed oddly out of perspective and very far away.

"Want to talk about Conor?" Greg said suddenly.

"Not really."

"He's quite the thing around here. Or so all the girls tell me."

"I wouldn't know," Martha said, and again had trouble reconciling her own impression of Conor with the female population of Bedford High.

"You two get along okay?"

Martha shrugged again. "I guess so." *We actually talked for the first time last night — does that count?*

"How about your dad? Your new stepmom — "

"They're in Hawaii. I haven't heard from them."

"Bet you miss them."

Martha shook her head. *I wouldn't give them the satisfaction.*

"You're not helping me out here, Martha," Greg said quietly, and Martha regarded him, almost pleading.

"What do you want me to say? I'm just . . . not catching on, that's all. I don't fit in."

"Have you tried?"

"The kids don't want to have anything to do with me — haven't you heard? I live in Elizabeth Bedford's house — "

"Martha, it's just a house. I can't believe you're — "

"Just a house?" Martha gave a twisted smile. "Right . . . where fires start and doors open and rooms never get warm — "

"Wait!" Greg put up his hands, but his laugh was strained. "What's all this about fires and doors and — ?"

"It's true," Martha said. "There's even a secret passageway behind my closet. Conor says there could be lots more we'll never even know about."

"That's probably somewhat true," Greg admitted. His glance was almost apologetic. "Martha, the house is over a century old — years ago it was used to hide runaway slaves. Elizabeth's father told me himself the place was supposed to be full of tunnels and secret rooms he'd heard about since he was a kid. There were even supposed to be ways to get from the house to the old cemetery out back — but the stories were probably exaggerated by the time they got to this generation. There probably weren't as many secret hiding places as there were rumors."

Martha wished she could feel as unconcerned about them as Greg seemed to feel. "And someone's been trying to scare me on the phone . . . calling me Elizabeth. . . ." She trailed off as Greg got up from his chair and stood at the window, running his fingers absently over his chin. It was several minutes before he spoke again. His voice sounded odd.

"People do weird things around Halloween. Do your folks know how you feel about the house?"

They don't care how I feel about anything. Aloud Martha said, "They love it there. I mean, they see all this great potential. . . . I guess I'm just unimaginative." She almost laughed at that.

"Okay, so maybe you shouldn't be in that house then. Maybe — at least for a while — you should stay with friends or something."

"I can't, don't you understand? I mean, there's nothing I'd like better than to never see that place again, but what can I do? Dad sure isn't gonna buy me a house of my own 'cause this one makes me crazy — "

Greg's shoulders straightened; he drew a deep breath and turned to face her, relaxed and conversational once more. "Martha, I'm sorry this house has become such a big issue with you. I wish you'd never heard any of the rumors at all. I mean, all these coincidences are unfortunate, but you shouldn't take them so seriously — it's really affecting other areas of your life. You obviously don't feel well, and your grades belong on somebody else's report card." He trailed one finger along the windowsill and wiped the dust carefully on his sleeve. "I'll be glad to talk to your dad about this when he — "

"Don't even bother," Martha sighed. "He wouldn't take you seriously anyway." She propped her chin in her hands, her face gloomy. "He doesn't understand why I don't like it. He probably wouldn't even understand why *Wynn* doesn't like it." Then catching herself, she dropped her eyes. "Sorry . . . I shouldn't have said that."

Greg smiled sympathetically. "You've been good for Wynn, Martha. It's nice to see her smile for a change." And then his own smile faded . . . tightened into a questioning look. "I don't suppose . . . she's talked to you about what happened that night?"

Martha shook her head. "She told me she can't remember things; that's all."

Greg sighed, gave a vague nod. "Well . . . what else can we do, huh? Other than that 'long dark' she keeps dreaming about, I guess she won't remember anything else till she's ready."

Martha looked thoughtful. "And you don't have any idea what that means — the long dark?"

"No." He offered a sad smile, shrugged his shoulders. "It was storming that night, and the house was so dark. I guess that's what keeps coming back to her . . . her long walk up the stairs to Elizabeth's room . . . or maybe she just blacked out for a second when she saw her. . . . It's hard to say. In her state of panic, a second could have seemed like an eternity."

Martha couldn't hold it in anymore. "Do *you* think Dennis drowned?" she blurted out.

"Of course," he said, and his eyes were calm and full upon her face. "Of course he drowned. They found some of his clothes miles downriver from here. Nobody's ever doubted that."

Blake does . . . I do. . . .

"Martha, I hate to see you borrowing trouble. You have enough to cope with right now — you don't need to invent new things." His smile was back again, warm, sympathetic, understanding. He stopped beside her and laid a hand on her shoulder. "You can talk to me anytime you want. Every day if you like. That's what I'm here for."

Martha nodded mechanically. If she stayed a second longer, she feared she'd burst into tears and never be able to face him again. Greg scrawled something on a piece of paper, folded it, and handed it over.

"I don't want to see you unhappy," he said. "Things don't have to stay this way."

If you'd get your act together, that's what you really mean. Martha closed the door behind her and headed slowly for class. She felt bruised — as if the weight of the world had finally come crashing down. And she felt humiliated — never in all her years of school had a teacher had to talk to her about her grades.

Wynn was waiting by her locker at the end of the day, and Martha gave her a rueful smile. "Congratulate me. I just wrote another paper on the wrong book."

"Oh, Martha, no. . . ." Wynn looked properly devastated, and Martha squeezed her arm.

"*And* I got lectured by *Mister* Chambers. It's been a full day."

"I'm sorry, Martha — and after all the reading you did, too."

Martha nodded tiredly. "If I don't get a decent grade in history next week, I might as well kill myself. If I don't, Dad will when he gets home."

"I could help you," Wynn said quietly. "With that report."

Martha turned and stared. "You're sweet . . . but you can't give the speech for me."

"No, but I could help you write it 'cause I've already read that book for another class. And maybe . . ." she hesitated, almost embarrassed, "I could come to your house and we could start studying together." As Martha stared at her, Wynn's cheeks grew pink. "If . . . if that's okay."

"Wynn, are you sure? I mean . . . really? You know I'd *love* you to come, but if you feel at all funny about it, I'll understand perfectly — "

"No," Wynn shook her head emphatically. "I want to. It's time, and I want to."

Martha nodded slowly, a mischievous smile going across her face. "I'll make sure Conor's home when you come."

This time Wynn's cheeks went crimson. "Oh, Martha, you wouldn't — please don't say anything — I — "

"Relax. He's weird, but I don't think he bites."
Martha laughed. "And I won't say anything. But I
still don't see what you see in him."

Now it was Wynn who looked surprised. "Why
Martha, he's so — so tall and rugged and mysterious — "

"He's not rugged. He's too thin to be rugged."

"He's rugged," Wynn insisted. "Lean and
strong — "

"How would you know?" Martha couldn't help
teasing.

"He *looks* strong. His shoulders look strong."

"I'll bet Blake is stronger."

"I'll bet he's not. All the girls say how sexy Conor
is."

"How would *they* know?"

"Well, look at Blake. He's too — well, *friendly*
to be sexy. No mystery there. Conor's the strong,
silent type."

"He's not always silent. Actually sometimes he's
pretty funny . . . in a sarcastic kind of way."

"Do you think *Blake's* sexy?"

"I'll bet he kisses better than Conor."

"I'll bet he doesn't."

They collapsed in helpless giggles and for a while
neither of them could speak. Finally Wynn caught
her breath and sagged back against Martha's locker.

"Oh, I hurt! I feel like some hot chocolate. You
don't have to go home right now, do you?"

"Well, I — " Martha broke off and grinned.
Conor was coming towards them down the hall,
seemingly oblivious to the female stares that fol-

lowed him. "Well, speak of the devil." She tried to compose herself as he stopped right beside a flustered Wynn. "I was just coming to find you," she said casually "You remember Wynn, don't you?"

"The picture hooks. Sure." Conor looked down, his face suggesting a smile. "Hi, Wynn, how are you?"

Wynn seemed to be having trouble catching her breath, but managed a quiet "Hi" in return. Martha rushed to fill the silence.

"Wynn and I have some things to do — could you pick me up later?"

"He doesn't have to do that," Wynn said. "One of us can give you a ride home."

"I've got to go to the library anyway," Conor said. "Where do you want me to meet you?"

"Here's okay, I guess."

"In the lot then. You have a watch?"

She held up her arm. "Five or so?"

He nodded, started to turn away, then caught himself absentmindedly. "You should come out to the house sometime, Wynn. Nice seeing you again."

"You, too." Wynn looked slightly breathless, and Martha didn't know whether to laugh or be sick.

"What *is* it about him?" she muttered, and as Wynn looked meaningfully at her, they both burst out laughing again. "I guess I just don't see it."

"It's hard," Wynn sighed, "when the boys in your family are more popular than you are."

"But you *must* see something in Blake!"

"What all the fuss is about?" Wynn made a face. "Handsome, athletic, charming, the celebrity of the

140

school — the *town* — and he's so *nice*, too! Except to me!"

"Come on," Martha teased, "you're crazy about him and you know it. But he must have a flaw."

"Only one," she nodded. "He likes to win. Now come on" — she hooked her arm through Martha's, and they headed out into the dismal weather — "let's get that hot chocolate and you can tell me more about Conor."

The steamy warmth of the coffee shop felt good. After they ordered hot drinks and settled back in their booth, Wynn leaned across the table conspiratorially.

"I hear you're going to the Halloween dance Sunday with Blake."

"How did you know that?"

"He told me. I think it's nice, too."

"Maybe we could go together," Martha suggested and was surprised when Wynn shook her head.

"I don't have a date. But thanks."

"Oh, Wynn — since you're on the decorating committee, I just assumed — "

"It's okay, really. I'm supposed to be in charge of the refreshments, so I wouldn't have time to dance. Anyway, it's good that I'm going. I need to do that." She tried to smile, but her mouth looked oddly frozen. "We all need to."

"Wynn," Martha said hesitantly, "Blake told me about what happened last year. About you finding Elizabeth and . . . well, he didn't want me to talk

141

about it with you, but I thought you should know that I know."

"He's always worrying about me," Wynn said sadly, "but if he really cared, he wouldn't keep saying that Dennis killed her. Because I know he didn't."

"I think," Martha said carefully, "that you're the only one who feels that way."

"I know. But it's true."

"But what about all the threats he made?" Martha persisted, not unkindly. "The phone calls and — "

"The phone calls she got — the person always disguised his voice. And all the times she thought he was following her, she couldn't see him clearly — she couldn't ever be sure it was Dennis." Wynn blinked back sudden tears. "Martha, I told you, he *loved* Elizabeth. He wanted her back, not to kill her. Oh, *damn* — I wish I could remember that night!" She bounced back angrily against the seat, and Martha reached out for her hand.

"What *do* you remember about that night?"

Wynn's eyes gazed desperately at the ceiling, then lowered back to Martha's face. They were narrowed now, almost painful in their concentration. "I know I found Elizabeth in her room — and all the blood — I remember — " She caught her breath, then forced herself on. "I remember Blake and Greg running up the stairs, shouting, and. . . ."

"And . . . what?" Martha asked gently.

Wynn's stare grew round and solemn. "The dark," she said flatly.

"What dark?"

"I . . just . . . the long dark! And I couldn't see . . . and it lasted forever . . . *so cold* . . . but *I can't remember*."

They looked up guiltily as the waitress set down their drinks. Wynn laced her hands around her cup and stared at the table.

"You never get over something like that," Martha murmured.

"No. I think about her every single day." Wynn glanced up, her voice trembling. "Dennis, too."

"But why?" Martha asked urgently. "Why does Blake feel so differently about Dennis?"

"He never saw Dennis with Elizabeth like I did . . . and she told me things . . . about the two of them. Most people couldn't get close to Dennis — but he could be sweet and gentle. . . ." A faint smile came at the memory. "He was handsome and kind of wild — he was romantic. He made her feel special, that's exactly what she told me. He made her feel special."

Martha closed her eyes, struggling to reconcile the two opposite images. *"She* must have known, then. I mean you *share* things in a relationship that no one else can share — "

"Blake *never* liked Dennis. It went back a long way. When Blake was a freshman, he made all-conference in basketball, and second team all-state. It was almost certain he'd make first team all-state his sophomore year. Then Dennis transferred here from another school. The coach was *ecstatic* 'cause Dennis had such a great reputation already — all

Coach could think about were these two superstars being teammates the next three years."

"So you're saying Blake was jealous of Dennis?"

Wynn frowned. "Blake had played against him twice when they were freshmen — he said Dennis was a dirty player." Reluctantly she nodded. "He was probably right about that — Dennis was a real hothead. He could be a terrible show-off, and he liked to take over. So Blake wasn't thrilled about him coming to Bedford. And then Dennis made all-state that year, but Blake didn't."

"So there really was a rivalry between them."

"After a while Blake started accusing Dennis of trying to injure him on the court. Like . . . when Blake was up in the air, Dennis would get under him as he came down so Blake would hurt his ankle. Blake's always had his heart set on a scholarship — if he got hurt and couldn't play. . . ."

"Then Dennis would have more chances to score. Not to mention more exposure and a better reputation."

Wynn gave a weary sigh. "That part could have been true, too. I know Blake's not a liar. But that was between Blake and Dennis — it had nothing to do with Elizabeth. Dennis was different with her. He wouldn't have hurt her."

"Wynn. . . ." Martha leaned slowly forward, her eyes glued to Wynn's troubled face. "I'm sorry but I've got to ask this — I have to know. What . . . do *you* think happened to Dennis?"

To her distress, Wynn suddenly began to cry. She buried her face in her hands and sobbed softly, and Martha grabbed her arms, her own heart wrenching.

"I think he's dead, Martha. . . . I think he killed himself."

Martha's expression froze, horror and sadness in every line. "Oh, Wynn — but — how — ?"

"I think when he heard she was dead, he just gave up. He told her once that he couldn't live without her — she *told* me he said that, and at the time we laughed 'cause it sounded so dramatic — oh, Martha, I'm so sorry now that I laughed — "

"Ssh . . . Wynn . . . drink this, it'll make you feel better." Martha's hands were shaking badly but she managed to guide the cup to Wynn's mouth, then gulp her own drink down. The melted marshmallows hit her stomach like rocks. Fighting down a pang of nausea, Martha forced her eyes away from Wynn and stared out into the late afternoon. The empty street gleamed wetly; the sidewalks were deserted. A traffic light blinked, turning puddles into pools of dark red blood. . . .

Her eyes went wide.

Stiffening, she pressed her nose against the glass and squinted hard, trying to see beyond the gray pall of rain. Then she wiped steam from the windowpane and looked again, a slow chill crawling over her.

She thought she'd seen something just then. . . .

Something caught between the shafts of pale light that speckled the sidewalk . . . something that had been there for a long time, like an image on the very edge of consciousness not quite formed. . . .

Is somebody there?

"It's hot in here," Martha mumbled. "I need some air." And before Wynn could say a word, Martha put some money on the table, excused herself, and stepped out onto the sidewalk. The street lay before her, rainwashed and silent. A long, slow breath of wind trailed soggy leaves through the gutter, and she stepped back from them as if they were alive.

There was no one out here.

The quiet was almost unnatural. . . .

"Martha?"

"Oh, God, Wynn, you gave me a heart attack." Martha fell back against her friend, gasping.

"Sorry — are you okay? I was getting worried."

"I thought — " Martha's eyes darted nervously up the street, probing, finding nothing. "I just thought I was going to faint for a second. I'm okay now."

"We'd better go then. Now that I've ruined our afternoon."

"Wynn! You didn't ruin anything! I never should have asked those questions — it's all my fault."

"It's not your fault. It's just all messed up. *I'm* all messed up — "

Martha laughed, throwing an arm around her shoulders. "*You're* not messed up. *We're* all messed up."

At that Wynn gave in to a chuckle. "Poor us."

"Yes. Poor us. And besides that, it's really getting cold out here now."

"I know," Wynn said dismally, pulling up the

hood of her jacket. "Oh, well, at least we don't have far to go."

Small comfort, Martha thought uneasily, and she plodded alongside Wynn without speaking. They'd gone about three blocks when Wynn suddenly stopped and turned.

"What is it?" Martha demanded.

"I'm not sure." Wynn looked puzzled, then shrugged. "I thought . . . oh, nothing." But she glanced back over her shoulder as they started walking again.

"Wynn?" Martha said stubbornly, and Wynn gave her a sheepish grin.

"Crazy — I thought I heard footsteps. But there's nobody back there. It was probably just some leaves or something. Before you know it, I'll be imagining Mr. Smith's mannequin is coming after us." At Martha's bewildered look, she giggled. "Mr. Smith's mannequin — back there. Didn't you see it? He always has it out in front of his store and takes it back in about this time every day."

Oh, great, I almost had hysterics over a dummy. . . . Martha forced a laugh. "Hey, *I'm* supposed to be the one with the overactive imagination, not you."

Wynn nodded, but they exchanged nervous glances and began moving in a half trot towards school.

"Do you see Conor?" Wynn asked.

Martha shook her head, a strange dread growing in the pit of her stomach. "He'll be here. You don't have to wait."

"Don't be silly, I — oh, *darn!*" Wynn checked her watch and looked helplessly at Martha. "I'm supposed to *baby-sit*, for crying out loud — "

"Then go on — Conor'll be here any second, I'm sure."

"Martha, I'm not leaving you alone."

"I'm a big girl," Martha chided, giving her a push. "I have to go in and get some stuff from my locker anyway. I'll wait under the overhang — I won't even get wet."

"Are you sure?" Wynn asked worriedly. "I mean, Bedford's not like Chicago, I don't think — we *can* go out at night alone here without guns . . . well . . . most of the time — "

"Get out of here," Martha laughed, waving her away. "I'll talk to you later."

"Are you *sure* Conor remembers you're here?"

"Wynn — *good-bye.*"

"Okay, then — " Wynn took off at a run, pausing at the corner to turn and wave. " 'Bye!"

" 'Bye." Martha stood there with her hand up, rain trickling down her cheeks, running into her collar.

"I think he's dead, Martha. . . . I think he killed himself. . . ."

She looked back at the school, looming against a starless sky, and her blood chilled within her. *Wynn . . . come back . . . please don't leave me alone. . . .*

Chapter 14

The heavy doors groaned as Martha swung them open.

She hadn't even considered that she might not get in — with football practice and drama rehearsals and club meetings going on, she felt confident that someone would still be here in some part of the building.

Anything was better than waiting outside in the dark . . . and now the rain had turned into a steady downpour. . . .

She hurried towards the stairs at the closest end of the hall. Funny how different everything seemed after school hours: classrooms empty, corridors uncomfortably oversized and damp and cold — and everything echoed — each step she took across the floor, each breath she breathed — all thrown mockingly back at her from the high old ceilings and peeling green walls. Martha quickened her pace and tried not to look at the gaping rooms on either side as she passed. *I guess I was wrong . . . there doesn't seem to be anyone around. . . .*

The staircase, just ahead of her now, angled upwards into murky shadows. Martha stopped at the bottom, biting her lip. She *had* to study this weekend for Tuesday's history discussion; if she didn't pull her grade up, she'd really be in serious trouble — not to mention the lecture she was sure to get from Dad — *and* Greg Chambers. She couldn't believe she'd been so dumb as to go off without her book in the first place. . . .

She sighed, glancing up to the second story. There was no choice, really — whether she wanted to or not, she had to go up there to her locker and get that stupid book.

She'd just put one foot on the bottom stair when she heard the sound.

Martha froze, her hand outstretched for the banister, and for one crazy minute she thought *she'd* made the sound herself because it was so *close* —

A footstep.

As light as a whisper, yet so unmistakable that the hair began to rise along the back of her neck.

It was just behind her.

With a gasp Martha whirled, her mouth open to scream —

The hall was empty.

Stunned, she gazed in disbelief at the black, endless corridor, her heart bursting in her ears. She groped for the railing and took a step up. The sound echoed like a gunshot.

There's no one here, Martha, it's just the old building or the wind or maybe mice in a closet somewhere or rats. . . . She shuddered and started up, angling her body so she could still see the hallway below. Even beneath her slight weight the old wooden stairs groaned and creaked — she couldn't remember it ever having taken so long to walk upstairs before.

Gratefully she reached the second floor, the dirty overhead lights illuminating rows of metal lockers lining the walls. With a relieved sigh, Martha headed towards her own locker, casting a last backwards look at the staircase as she grabbed her lock and began to spin the combination. *It's a good thing Conor isn't here to see me . . . I'd never live this down.* . . . She pulled out her history book and gave herself a firm mental shake. This place was really creepy; it was too easy to imagine all kinds of horrors. Well, this would be *her* little secret — no sense letting anyone know how a creaky old building had sent her into a near panic. Smiling at her own silliness, Martha slammed the door.

The hall plunged into total darkness.

In the first split second she felt more surprise than fear — one minute she was heading for the stairs; in the next breath she was pinned against the lockers, the suffocating darkness worse than any darkness she had ever known. She couldn't even see the book in her hand or the fingers she put up to her lips to press back the scream forming there. . . .

She couldn't see a thing.

But she could hear the footsteps . . . slow . . . purposeful . . . climbing the stairs.

For one insane instant Martha felt hope leap inside her — she actually thought the janitor was making his rounds in the dark.

"Hello!" Martha called. "I forgot a book in my locker — could you turn the lights back on?"

Nobody answered.

Martha felt her heart sink deep into the frozen pit of her stomach. "Oh, no," she whispered.

The footsteps stopped.

And waited.

And then, hesitantly, they started again.

Martha's eyes, wild with terror, were totally useless to her now — as she moved cautiously from her locker, she waited for hands to grab her, hands that were used to the dark . . . the hallway swarming with hands. . . .

The footsteps kept coming — one stair at a time — unhurried and unconcerned.

As if they knew right where they were going.

Martha swallowed a sick taste of fear.

The footsteps reached the second floor.

They didn't stop. They came straight towards her.

Some mechanism took over then — some instinct for self-preservation — before Martha even realized what was happening, she was stumbling through the darkness, away from him. She put out her hands, groping — *Think, Martha, think!* There was another stairway at the opposite end of the hall — if she could just reach it — run down and get outside — find Conor — The enormity of the situation suddenly overwhelmed her — in terror she felt her fingers slide over a light switch and she hit it — again — again — *my God, he's cut off the power*.

Desperately she began to run, legs numb, clumsy with fear. She didn't care anymore if he heard her or not — all she knew was she had to get out of there —

She hit a wall, fought to keep her balance. And still the footsteps came, never changing their pace. *The stairs — the stairs!* She knew she'd reached the end of the hall and the stairs should be to her left — flinging her arms she suddenly hit double doors. She threw herself against them, pounding on the handles, but they wouldn't budge. Whimpering, she slid down the wall, her fist rammed into her mouth. Behind her the footsteps halted, blocking her escape.

Where *was* he? How far behind her? Yet she could *sense* that he was close — *so close!* — and she wondered crazily where there was left to run —

Later she couldn't remember diving for the open classroom — later she was astounded that she'd even remembered it was there at all — but suddenly she was throwing herself through the door and slamming it, and falling over furniture before she finally found the back windows that opened out onto the fire escape.

She tugged at the bottom section of glass.

The window stuck fast.

Behind her the doorknob turned and the door began to open.

Martha ducked down behind some desks, molding herself as flat as she could to the wall. The feet came slowly into the room and stopped. The silence was endless and terrifying. She pressed both hands to her mouth to keep from screaming.

And then he closed the door.

Martha heard the groan of the hinges and knew that she was completely and hopelessly trapped. There was no way out now, except to go right past him, and now there was only the silence again . . . endless . . . agonizing . . . silence . . . and her heart splitting her body with convulsions of terror.

His hand came out of nowhere.

It sprang from the darkness and clamped down on her shoulder, and with a shriek Martha broke away from him and hurled herself where she thought the door should be. Her hand grappled with the knob — the door strained for a brief instant — stuck — then popped open, spilling her out into the hall.

Behind her he swore under his breath.

And began to run.

Martha beat frenziedly upon the doors that blocked the stairway. Without warning they suddenly came open, and she pitched forward, missing the banister. Her arm made an awful cracking sound as she landed on it. Then, half running, half falling, she somehow got to the bottom and ran for the nearest exit, throwing her weight against the door.

It was locked.

No . . . no . . . God . . . no. She was crying now; the pain in her arm excruciating.

And now she heard him, behind her, on the stairs. . . .

She screamed — screamed again — the pain like a ragged knife in her arm, up her shoulder — screaming, praying somebody would hear —

She was almost past her last chance when she remembered.

The side door that led off through the teachers' lounge, that none of the students were ever allowed to use. . . .

Martha turned the corner so abruptly she nearly fell again. She pulled herself along the walls, and heard the footsteps falter, confused by her sudden turn.

The white-hot pain burned through her whole body — she went down on one knee, hugging her arm against her. Her shoulder hit the door as she wrestled with the metal bar that would open it — as the door burst open she felt the cold shock of wind and rain and a different kind of darkness — a paler darkness — where streetlights glowed through fog, throwing puddles of distorted light —

"Conor!" she screamed. *"Conor!"*

Behind her the door burst open.

Martha screamed and ran, mindlessly now, only knowing she had to get away.

"Conor!"

Miraculously, through tears and rain she saw the parking lot. And as the familiar station wagon came into view with its interior light on, Martha was suddenly conscious of two things —

The station wagon was empty.

And the footsteps behind her had stopped.

As reality began to flood her terrified brain, she collapsed against a light post, eyes wide and dull, staring at the empty car. The headlights beamed hazily through the night.

"Conor — " she tried to call, but no sound would come. She looked behind her, and saw a black silhouette slide back into the darkness.

"Oh . . . help me. . . ." Martha suddenly felt faint. As she groped for the post, her legs turned to jelly and began to buckle. She saw the wet gleaming pavement rushing up towards her face — she threw up her hands in slow motion and waited for the impact —

"Martha!"

And she *knew* that voice, it was Conor's voice, coming out of nowhere, out of the dark. . . .

And she felt his arms beneath her . . . saw his eyes . . . and then she felt nothing, falling into the deep, smothering night.

Chapter 15

"It hurts."

"Of course it hurts. You nearly twisted your arm off."

Martha groaned and tried to raise her head. "Conor — "

"No, we can't leave till the doctor says we can." He watched the confusion on her face and added, "You remember where you are, don't you? You drifted off again just now."

Martha stared at him for a moment, then without warning her face crumpled and she began to cry.

"Hey — " Conor came to the bedside, patting her shoulder awkwardly. "Martha, come on now, don't — "

"But somebody tried to kill me," Martha sobbed. "Don't you believe me?"

Conor regarded her unhappily, but before he could answer a nurse leaned through the doorway, giving them a smile.

"You can take her home in a little bit — the doctor wants to give her a prescription."

"Thanks," Conor said, and looked down again as the nurse left.

"I don't want to go home," Martha cried softly, and the throbbing in her arm squeezed her whole body. "Please, Conor — "

"Martha." Conor sat down on the side of her bed, his eyes clear and troubled. "I called the police after I brought you here. They didn't find anyone, and they didn't take me very seriously."

"Of course they didn't find anyone — he ran away when he saw your car. Where *were* you?"

"I told you before," Conor said patiently. "When you didn't show up on time, I got worried and went to look for you. I couldn't get in 'cause the doors were all locked and — " He broke off at the sudden commotion in the hall, and a moment later Blake and Greg came hurrying into the room.

"Martha! Are you okay? What the hell happened?"

"Blake, what are you doing here?" Martha looked confused as she wiped clumsily at her eyes.

"They told us you were in here — I didn't believe it." Blake leaned over the bed and stared at her cast.

"What *are* you doing here?" Conor asked quietly. He stood his position by her bed, and something in his voice caused Martha to look at him curiously.

Greg moved to the other side of her pillow and peered earnestly into her face, his smile sympathetic. "Boy, kiddo, when you have a run of bad luck, you really go all the way, don't you?"

"You're not supposed to be in here," Conor said.

Blake barely gave him a glance as he crowded in and took Martha's free hand. "Are you okay? Are you hurt bad?"

Martha fought the sedation, but it was hard to think clearly. "I . . . I fell down the stairs — "

"Where? Did you break anything else?"

"She shouldn't be talking," Conor said. "She needs to rest. I'm taking her home."

"I don't want to go home," Martha said automatically. "Someone's trying to hurt me."

"Martha — " Conor began, but Blake cut him off.

"What are you talking about?" He sat down on the edge of the bed, nudging her over. "*Who's* trying to hurt you?"

"Someone was following me." Martha blinked, trying to keep things in focus. "And someone turned out the lights and followed me."

"She's not up to this right now," Conor interrupted, but Blake jumped up.

"I'm calling the police."

"I already did that."

"Wait a minute." Greg put out his hands, motioning Blake back down. "What about the lights?"

"He turned them off." Martha tried to sit up, straining against Blake's arms. "The lights went off and he — "

"Martha," Greg said gently, "there was a power failure tonight. Because of the rain. The lights were off all over town for a little while."

Martha stared, her eyes glazed. "They went out

". . ." she murmured, "they went out because he turned them off. . . . Conor, tell them I didn't dream it — "

Blake coaxed her down again, staring with grave concern. Greg glanced over at Conor, then nodded towards the hall.

"Can I talk to you for a minute?"

They walked out to the waiting room, and for several moments Greg paced, frowning down at the floor. Finally he stopped and looked at Conor. Conor slid his hands into his back pockets and waited.

"Look," Greg drew a deep breath, "maybe I should have said something before now. I understand your folks are out of town."

Conor nodded.

"Well, the truth is, Martha's under a lot of stress. She's doing terrible at school."

"I think she knows that."

"Not that it's so abnormal — new family, new school — new peer group. I'm not saying she's imagining what happened tonight — but the last time she talked to me, she was really upset about your house. Going on about secret passageways and fires and — "

"It's a strange house," Conor said. "It has lots of . . . inconsistencies."

"I understand." Greg looked down at the floor again, his tone guarded. "Look, I'll be glad to do what I can to help her through this rough time — but . . . you might consider professional help. . . ."

Conor nodded, rocking back on his heels. A muscle worked in his jaw. "Martha's fine," he said.

"Yeah . . . well. . . ." Greg straightened and glanced at the clock on the wall. "I've gotta get to work. I'm on a teen hotline here at the hospital two nights a week — Blake gave me a lift over." He backed towards a doorway that led off to another hall. "You might talk it over with your parents. If I can do anything. . . ." He left the offer unfinished. Conor stared after him, then went back into Martha's room.

The next day was Saturday, and Martha slept off her pain pills till almost noon. When she finally woke up, she was in Conor's old room and there was a loud chorus of coughing and hammering coming from the side of the house. She dragged herself to the window; Conor smiled in at her from atop a ladder and stuffed a handkerchief back into his pocket.

"Uh-oh. It's *alive*."

"Very funny, Conor. What time is it?"

"Late. You almost slept the day away. How's your arm?"

Martha frowned down at her cast, but she wasn't thinking about her broken bones. *I almost slept the day away . . . and now it's almost tomorrow . . . almost Halloween. . . .*

"Martha?" Conor asked softly.

"What are you doing up here anyway?" Martha groaned. "Don't you have any respect for the injured?"

"I promised your dad I'd have these shutters fixed before he got home and — " He broke off abruptly, sneezed, then glanced back over his shoulder.

"What is it? Besides the fact that you're spraying me with cold germs?"

"I think we have a visitor."

"Who?"

"I think it's Wynn."

"You're kidding — " From where she stood, Martha couldn't see anything, only Conor waving at someone and telling them to go inside. Gritting her teeth against the pain, Martha started downstairs and saw Wynn step hesitantly into the lower hall. As Martha stood there watching, her heart ached within her. Wynn looked absolutely terrified.

"Wynn," Martha called softly.

The girl jumped, her face paling slightly. "Martha — I heard what happened last night — I feel so awful about it — "

"Don't." Martha brandished her cast and winced. "I was just in the wrong place at the wrong time."

"I shouldn't have left you — "

"I shouldn't have gone in." Martha smiled grimly. "I'm gonna look great for the party tomorrow night. Come on up. You're just in time to help wrestle me into my clothes."

Wynn nodded and started up, her hand gripped white on the banister, her eyes darting nervously. Below them the front door opened and Conor stood quietly, watching. As Wynn reached the landing she stared in silence at the doorways, at the servants' hall, and then without a word she headed straight for the back bedroom.

Martha caught her gently by the arm. "Not there. I'm in this room now."

"This one?" Wynn's face registered slow surprise. "Oh . . . I . . . I'm so used to going to Elizabeth's room. . . ."

"I *did* have that room, but I just feel too weird about it. So Conor's trading with me. I still have to move my stuff in here, though."

Wynn nodded and followed her inside, her eyes roving over Conor's sparse assortment of belongings as Martha gathered up some clothes.

"So," Martha said with forced cheerfulness, "how did you get out here anyway?"

"I borrowed Greg's car."

"How did you manage that?"

"He doesn't know about it yet."

Martha laughed. "Have you had lunch? I feel really hungry today, but the way Conor's been coughing around here, he'll probably give me his cold and — "

Wynn wasn't listening, her gaze sweeping the hall beyond the door. Martha watched her sadly and sighed.

"Wynn, really, I can't stand this. It must be so hard for you to come back in here — to remember — if you want to leave, I'll understand."

"No." The adamance of her tone surprised Martha, and Wynn looked back at her, unflinching. "No, this is something I have to do. If I don't get all this figured out, I'll have to spend my whole life with a blank page in my mind." She took a step forward, her eyes wide and solemn. "Martha, yesterday you asked me what I thought happened to Dennis. Why . . . why did you ask me that?"

For a long moment Martha couldn't even speak. Wynn's eyes held her in a relentless stare, and though her lips parted, no answer formed. When Conor spoke from the doorway they both started.

"What are the chances," Conor asked casually, "of Dennis still being alive?"

At first Martha thought Wynn might faint. Her face drained the last of its color, and she groped out blindly for Martha's hand. Martha sat her down on the edge of the bed and motioned for Conor to raise the window.

"I . . . I . . . alive?" Wynn murmured.

"Yes." Conor knelt before her, his voice urgent but kind. "They never found him, they never proved anything — it's *possible*, isn't it, Wynn? That if he was crazy enough to kill Elizabeth, that he could still be out there, thinking somehow that she's still alive?"

Martha collapsed in a chair. *He said it.* After all the days of fear and confusion, the questions, the *terror* — thinking all along that maybe it was *her* — that *she* was the crazy one — Conor had finally come out and said it. She looked at him and her eyes blurred, but he had hold of Wynn's hands and didn't see her.

"Wynn," he said again, softly, "it is possible, isn't it?"

Wynn looked confused, then shook her head sorrowfully. "I'd know . . . if Dennis were back, I'd *know* about it."

"How?" Conor persisted. "How would you know?"

"I . . . I just . . ." She stopped, took a deep breath, squared her shoulders. "I think he'd try to contact me somehow. To find out what happened, to see if it was safe. He *always* talked to me about Elizabeth because he knew how close we were. And he didn't kill her. I know he didn't."

"But *how* do you know that?" Conor squeezed her hands. "How can you be sure? He threatened her and — "

"He just didn't want her going out with Blake, that's all. Any more than Blake wanted her going back to him. It just really infuriated him that Blake had her now — they'd always been such rivals — girls and basketball and honors and scholarships — " She shook her head, pressing her hands to her temples.

"So Dennis was pretty possessive of Elizabeth?"

Wynn gave a reluctant nod.

"And had a bad temper."

A pause. Another nod.

"So they *could* have had an argument. He *could* have lost his head and done something violent."

Wynn looked miserably at the floor. "I . . . guess so. But couldn't anyone have done that? I mean, couldn't he have found out she'd been killed and then killed himself? Or couldn't it have been a coincidence that his car went off the bridge and he died? Or couldn't the same person who killed Elizabeth have killed him, too?"

Conor and Martha exchanged looks.

"Wynn," Martha said gently, "anything is possible, but those are pretty farfetched — "

"Not any more farfetched than calling Dennis a murderer." Wynn's voice was desperate now, and she met Conor's eyes at last. "Don't you see I have to try to remember for Dennis's sake? After all the doctors I went to, trying to jar my memory, and then I figured this house was out of my life forever, and I'd *never* remember again. But then you came here — and Martha's so much like Elizabeth — and now the house is back in my life again — and it's all so strange and scary — like this was *meant* to be — like Elizabeth and Dennis did this on purpose 'cause they *want* me to help them prove what really happened. . . ." She trailed off, looking pleadingly into Conor's eyes. "It . . . sounds so silly. . . ."

"No." Conor released her hands, a reassuring smile at the corners of his lips. Reassuring and *worried*, Martha thought . . . *he looks so tired.* . . . "No, it isn't silly," Conor said again. "We'll help you."

The gratitude on Wynn's face was heartrending. Conor stood and ran one hand absently through his hair. "I'll make us lunch. We can talk some more downstairs."

After much tugging and pulling Wynn finally managed to help Martha get dressed, and they met down in the kitchen where Conor was serving up soup and sandwiches. At first Wynn only picked at her food, but as Conor drew her out about school and her job at the store, Martha could see her beginning to relax a little. And when he finally did steer the talk back to the matter at hand, Martha couldn't help but marvel at his skillful subtlety. He stood at the kitchen window, looking out at the dismal weather, and gave a loud sigh.

"Well, if this rain doesn't get any worse, I might be able to get more of those shutters fixed today. Oh, and I boarded up that panel in your closet, too, Martha."

"I thought you did that be — " Martha started without thinking, then caught the warning glance Conor tossed back over his shoulder.

Wynn frowned, twirling her spoon idly in her soup.

"That's probably what caused the drafts," Conor went on. "Made it so cold in that room and kept blowing the door open."

"Did you know that, Wynn?" Martha picked up casually. "That there's a secret door inside the closet in my old room?"

Wynn looked puzzled for a moment, as if she'd suddenly awoken in a room full of strangers. And then a light slowly began to dawn in her eyes. "Of course I know about it . . . only I hadn't thought about it all this time. There're supposed to be lots of secret tunnels and things in the house — Elizabeth's father said he'd heard stories about them since he was a little boy, but he only knew about a few."

Martha felt her pulse quicken, but Conor remained maddeningly calm. "Do you know where they are?"

For a split second Wynn looked blank, but then she nodded slowly. "We weren't allowed to use them — they were so old and Mr. Bedford was afraid we'd get hurt. In fact, he boarded up the one in Elizabeth's room, but — "

"But what?"

She looked almost embarrassed. "Elizabeth tore it down. So Dennis could use it."

"No fool, Dennis," Conor murmured. Louder he said, "Was Dennis the only other one who knew about the passages?"

Wynn glanced away uncomfortably. "And . . . Blake."

"Blake!" Martha exclaimed.

"Yes . . . when he and Elizabeth started going out, she told me she'd told him about them."

"You're sure about that," Conor said.

"That's what she said," Wynn insisted. "There was one . . . that went from the cellar to the study . . . and one from the attic to the pantry."

"Were there any that led outside?"

Again Wynn looked blank. "I don't know."

"Another way someone could get into the house?"

Wynn shook her head, close to tears. "I don't know — "

Conor put a hand on her shoulder. "It's okay," he said softly. "Take it easy. You're doing fine."

"I'm *not*," Wynn said hopelessly. "Oh, if I could only — "

"Okay," Conor said soothingly, "don't try so hard. Just relax." His voice was lulling . . . hypnotic. . . . "Tomorrow's Halloween . . . but let's go back. Halloween night a year ago. Can you see it? Is it too painful?"

"I . . . I don't think so. . . . I'll try. . . ." Wynn glanced nervously at Martha, who nodded encouragement, then she stared down at the table, her voice hesitant and shaking. "We all went to the party at school that night. Elizabeth was really mad 'cause she'd gotten another phone call. She said she'd had it with Dennis and his immature attitude and she was gonna do what she wanted. Blake was mad, too — hoping Dennis would be there so he could let him have it once and for all. But none of them were really taking it seriously — they weren't scared or anything. They just wanted to party and have a good time."

"So you were all there?"

"Yes — you don't really have to have a date or anything — but Blake and Elizabeth kind of made themselves scarce."

Martha tried to ignore the implication as Wynn shot her an apologetic look.

"We were supposed to unmask at midnight," Wynn went on.

"Wait a minute — " Conor stopped her. "It was a costume party?"

"Yes. They have one every year."

Conor leaned back against the counter, crossing his legs. "So did anybody actually see Dennis come in? Did they recognize him?"

Wynn nodded. "Yes. I did. He came up to me and asked if Elizabeth was there, and I said yes, that she was with Blake."

"What did he say to that?"

"Not much, just looked really mad about it. He

went off into the crowd and I didn't see him again for a while. Then Elizabeth and Blake had a fight."

"About what? Dennis?"

Wynn thought a moment. "I'm not sure — but Greg came up to me at the refreshment table and said Blake had stormed out of the gym."

"Alone?"

Wynn nodded. "We weren't supposed to be wandering around outside, so Greg went to look for him. He was gone pretty long — in the meantime I went to find Elizabeth, and I couldn't find her, either."

"Did she leave, too?"

"It was so dark in there — so many people — everyone had costumes on and so many of them looked alike. I looked and looked for her a long time, but I couldn't find her."

"What'd you do then?"

"I didn't know what to do. I was starting to get really scared. I finally went outside to find Greg — and that's when I saw them."

"Who?"

"Elizabeth and Dennis. In Dennis's car. They were pulling out of the parking lot, and I yelled at them, and Elizabeth leaned out the window and said they were only going to her house to talk and not to tell Blake 'cause he'd be mad. She said they needed to get something straight — and then they'd be right back."

"So . . . you covered for her."

Wynn looked miserable. "I lied to Greg. I told him Elizabeth had gotten sick and we were going to my house for a while — "

"And he never suspected?"

Wynn shook her head slowly. "The house was close by, and he was still trying to find Blake — *and* he was supposed to be chaperoning, too. Some of the guys got into a fight with the band, and there was a big commotion — so he wasn't really thinking too much about Elizabeth and me."

"Then you went home."

Wynn closed her eyes, took a deep breath. "My folks were out that night, so I hung around for a while — then I just went back to school and sat in Greg's car and waited for Elizabeth to come back."

"How long were you there?"

"About an hour, I guess, I'm not sure." She raised her eyes, pressed a hand to her forehead. "And then I saw Blake drive up in his car. . . . He looked . . . upset . . . and his clothes were all wet and he just sat there for a long time, like he was thinking."

"And Elizabeth still hadn't come back?"

"No. Finally Blake got out and went back into the gym and — I just didn't know what to do. I was really starting to panic by then. When I went in, Greg and Blake were waiting for me — I — I had to tell them the truth then, that she wasn't really with me — but she'd made me *promise* — " Her voice faltered. "I was so *scared* — so *scared* — suddenly all the stuff we'd laughed at seemed so — so *dangerous* — "

"So she'd been gone for more than an hour by then," Conor said. "And where had Blake been?"

Wynn looked down at her hands, twisted them

in her lap. "He said he'd driven around for a while —
then he'd just gotten out of his car and walked.
When he found out I'd let Elizabeth go like that, he
was *furious* — I've never seen him so mad —
he — " She covered her face with her hands and
began to cry. "Don't you understand now how awful
this is? *I'm* the one who saw them leave! I'm the
one who saw them, and I didn't *do* anything!"

"But you didn't know." Martha tried to comfort
her. "You couldn't have known — "

"But she *trusted* me! She asked me to cover for
her while she left with Dennis — she *trusted* me,
and I could have stopped her, and then she *died*!"

For a long while there was only the sound of
Wynn's sobs . . . the gloomy hiss of rain down the
window . . . the whine of wind around the eaves.
. . . Conor looked like a statue, his angular face
caught in the soft glow of the kitchen light. He
seemed to pull his thoughts together with an effort.

"What happened when you got here?" he asked
then. "When you got here to the house?"

The sobs faded. . . . From behind her hands
Wynn's voice was dull with pain. "It took us a long
time to get here. Blake was driving and we got a
flat tire. The boys were yelling at each other —
Blake was yelling at me — "

"So you're finally at the house now." Conor
reached down and gently raised Wynn from her
chair. "So what do you do now?"

Wynn hung back, her face ashen. Martha took
one of her hands, and gave her an encouraging
smile.

"It's all right. We'll go through it with you. It can't hurt you with us here, you know that."

Conor nodded; Martha could tell it was Conor who convinced Wynn at last. Wynn went slowly into the front hall. For several moments she stared at the heavy door, then lifted her chin determinedly.

"It was storming when we got here — Blake jumped out of the car before Greg even had it parked, and he started banging on the door and yelling. But the door was locked, and there was only one light on — back in Elizabeth's room. He just went crazy, beating and shouting — and Greg was trying to find a way in — " She squeezed her eyes shut, squeezing the vision from the past. "He broke one of the windows on the terrace. He put his hand through the glass and broke it, and we all got inside."

Very slowly, almost as if she were drugged, Wynn took a step forward . . . another . . . and another . . . and reached out for the banister.

"They were yelling at me to stay there — *Blake* was yelling at me not to go upstairs — 'Don't let her go up there' he kept saying, and Greg was trying to grab me, but I started *running* — I don't remember getting from the parlor to the stairs, but I did and . . . and. . . ."

"Go on," Conor said gently. "It's all right."

Wynn started up the staircase, her footsteps wooden and slow. Conor touched Martha on the elbow, and they followed.

"The light was on, but I couldn't see anyone,"

Wynn whispered. "And I think — I know — I called her name — "

Martha's heart felt ready to burst. Every nerve warned her to turn and flee, but Conor's hand gripped hold of her arm. She looked at him, but his eyes were on Wynn.

"She didn't answer me. And it was so *quiet* — even though Greg and Blake were yelling — calling me to come back — even with them shouting like that, it was just so . . . so *quiet* — and I kept saying her name, 'Elizabeth . . . *Elizabeth*,' but she wouldn't *answer*."

They had reached the second floor now. Wynn's hands went nervously to her throat, and Martha wondered if she was going to be sick.

"Conor, maybe this isn't such a good idea, maybe we — "

"Keep still, Martha," Conor whispered. "And then what happened?" he said more loudly to Wynn.

"I went into her room," Wynn said dully. After an uneasy pause, she moved forward until the three of them were squeezed into the door of Elizabeth's bedroom. Wynn stared ahead and Martha could tell that whatever she saw was horrible.

"You're in her room now," Conor murmured. "What do you see, Wynn?"

Wynn's eyes fell at once to the bed, and her face slowly began to drain. "I . . . she's lying there . . . her mouth is open but I can't hear her screaming . . . and the room is so red . . . red and wet . . . and . . . she doesn't look like Elizabeth anymore."

Martha's eyes blurred; she felt Conor's hand

tighten on her arm. His face was drawn, stony. Wynn started to turn back to where they were standing.

And then her eyes passed over the open closet.

Martha saw her stiffen and knew at once that something was wrong. Conor must have sensed it even sooner — she felt him turn loose of her as he started across the floor towards Wynn.

"What is it?" Conor demanded. "What do you see?"

And Wynn fell back, clutching at him, her eyes wide, her words tumbling out in a helpless sort of babble —

"The . . . the dark . . . it's so *long* — it's so — "

"*What*, Wynn, *what* dark? Did the lights go out that night?"

"It . . . it just lasts forever!" She spun around, panicky, her eyes huge with terror. "It just goes on and *on* — "

"How long? How long did the dark last? Wynn — try to — "

"No!" she cried. "I can't *remember*! The dark is so *long* and I *can't remember*!"

Chapter 16

"I'm sorry you're not going," Martha said. She frowned at her reflection in the mirror and heard Conor coughing from his bed.

"Don't tell me you might miss me," he choked.

"No, I might need protection."

"From Blake Chambers? I thought you didn't want protection from him."

Martha glanced back over her shoulder. "Don't laugh at me, Conor, it's not funny."

"Do I look like I'm laughing?"

"Your *face* isn't laughing, your *voice* is laughing."

"Then my voice must be in a better mood than the rest of me," he said wearily.

"It serves you right, and I don't feel a bit sorry for you. You should know better than to go around fixing shutters in the cold rain." Martha stole a glance at him, then adjusted her black shawl over her gypsy costume, trying to hide her cast. "Oh, Conor, what do you think Wynn means about 'the long dark'?"

Conor shook his head, tilted it back, trying to

breathe. "For the hundredth time, I don't know. Wynn can't remember, and it won't help to nag her about it."

"But it's Halloween." Martha looked pleading. "What if Dennis really *isn't* dead — what if he comes back tonight and — ?" She broke off, bit her lip. "It *could* be him, you know."

"It could be anyone," Conor said. He flung an arm restlessly across his forehead. "Look, you haven't gotten any more phone calls, have you?"

Martha shrugged and shook her head. "No . . . but that still doesn't explain what happened that night at school. That *wasn't* an accident — but I keep trying to convince myself it was — or that maybe whoever chased me thought I was someone else. But I don't believe it." She gave him a wry smile. "And you're just trying to make me feel better, aren't you? You're worried, too."

"I'm too sick to be worried." Conor stared at her, at the desperation in her eyes. "All right, I'm a *little* worried," he relented. "So that's it. I'm going." He tried to push back the covers, but Martha stopped him.

"Look at you — you're so weak you can't even climb out of bed, much less be my bodyguard." For the third time that evening she took a really hard look at him, and felt strangely uneasy. His face was like marble, and his eyes had a feverish brightness; his cheekbones jutted sharply beneath his skin, giving his face a ghostly sunkenness. She'd insisted he take his old room again because it was warmer, and then she'd piled blankets on him, but he was still shivering. Martha's lips moved — her conscience fought a quick battle — and lost. "I can't stay here, Conor. Please, *please* understand — I *can't* stay in this house tonight, I'm just so *scared* — "

He turned his face from her; she thought his head moved in a nod.

"Conor — I — " Martha's eyes filled with tears, and she wiped at them angrily. "I'll be with Blake all evening and then I'll spend the night at Wynn's — I'll leave her number in case you need me — "

"I won't need you."

Martha looked pleadingly at the back of his head, the damp hair tousled on the pillow. "I can't, Conor . . . I just can't stay — "

"Will you just leave then, so I can get some sleep?"

"You're just trying to make me feel guilty."

"I'm not trying to make you do anything except leave — " Conor began coughing again, waving her weakly away. "Go on. Get out of here."

Reluctantly Martha nodded, started out the door.

"Martha — "

She spun around. "Yes?"

"Be careful," he said quietly.

And she was glad she heard the car then, honking from the driveway. Without another word to Conor she hurried downstairs and out the front door.

"Blake! Hi!" Martha lifted up her long skirt and dodged the puddles as best she could, trying to hold her shawl over both her cast and her head at the same time. Rain, rain, and more rain — and from the looks of those boiling clouds, there would be another bad storm tonight. "Remind me to call Conor later, okay? He's really sick and — "

She broke off and stared.

Blake had turned off the headlights and the inside of the car was dark. What light there was came from the weak glow of the porchlight, barely trickling over the side of Blake's car.

But something was in his window.

Something hideous sat in the driver's seat and grinned at her fiendishly from the loose folds of a hooded cape.

"Blake — " Martha stammered. "What — ?"

"I'm Death," the thing said. And then it opened her door and beckoned. "Climb on in."

The gym had undergone a macabre transformation — dark to the point of obscurity, with only jack-o'-lanterns glowing from the tables and corners; it swarmed with strange unearthly creatures, all trying to keep their identities secret until the midnight unmasking.

After Martha's initial shock, Blake had removed the mask for the ride to town, but now both he and Martha were in complete disguises, weaving their way through the packed crowds, trying to find a place to sit. As Blake pulled out her chair, a huge axe descended slowly upon their table, and Martha let out a squeal, finding herself face to face with a black-hooded, black-robed executioner.

"Greg," Blake scoffed to Martha, "I'd know him anywhere."

The familiar voice inside the hood sounded disappointed. "And I thought I looked so different. Especially with my prop here."

"Yeah, well, you've never been known for your thinking," Blake threw back. "You mean they let you in with that thing?"

"Chaperone's prerogative," Greg said. "I get to use it on bad kids."

Blake laughed. "Anybody seen Wynn?"

"The witch over there serving the punch. Complete with missing teeth and warts on the nose. Here, Martha, have a souvenir." Greg leaned over, holding a match to one of the unlighted candles, then dropped the matchbook in Martha's lap.

"Poor Wynn," Martha slid the matchbook into her pocket, "will she have to do that all night?"

"What do you mean 'poor Wynn'?" Greg sounded offended. "*I* happen to be her date, you know."

"Sorry, Greg, but I think she would have preferred Conor," Martha laughed. "Except he's down with the flu or something."

"Uh-oh. Bad?"

"Pretty bad. But he'll be okay, I guess. He won't let me call the doctor, so there's not much I can do about it."

"And all the girls in Bedford High will be in mourning till he recuperates, no doubt. Blake, old man, you're definitely losing your touch with the female populace."

The black cape rustled, and one black-draped arm slid around Martha's shoulders. "On the contrary, I haven't lost a thing. I'm definitely a winner — and you know how I like to win."

Funny . . . that's what Wynn said about him. . . .

Blake tapped her lightly on her cast. "Hey, gypsy lady, how about a dance?"

"Just keep him in line," Greg advised her. "Put a curse on him if he gives you any trouble."

Martha laughed as Blake pulled her to the dance floor. The music was earsplitting and bodies were pressed so close together that it was hard to stay with one partner. *It could be anyone. . . .* Martha's eyes probed the pulsating darkness, the orange jack-o'-lantern grins laughing from the corners. Anyone could be in here, hiding, watching her, waiting. . . .

Damn you, Conor, you said that just to ruin my evening!

It could be anyone.

"Martha — "

"Oh, Wynn, you scared me to death!"

"Sorry — my clothes are so black, I kind of blend in, I guess. And no, I didn't recognize you, but I already saw Blake's costume — "

"You *made* my costume," Blake corrected her. "You made *all* our costumes — that's why they all look so much alike — "

"They're wonderful costumes," Martha laughed.

"Wynn, get out of here," Blake said, still trying to dance in spite of the interruption.

Wynn pointedly ignored him. "How's Conor?"

Another pang of guilt. Martha pushed it firmly away. "Actually he's miserable, but it's good for him. Makes him more sympathetic to the human condition. Hey, you sound kind of tired — are *you* okay?"

"Maybe it's going around." Wynn brushed her off. "Anyway, I was up all night and all today decorating this stupid place — I'll be glad when Halloween's over."

Something in Wynn's tone alerted Martha, the words that hadn't been spoken aloud: *Halloween — and the shadow of a tragedy.* Martha reached out for her friend's hand. "Why don't you come sit with us?"

"I don't believe this." Blake stopped dancing. "If I'd known you two wanted to come together — "

"I can't." Somewhere beneath the green witch face Wynn smiled. "I'm too busy pouring punch and keeping the trays filled to visit — but stop by the table sometime."

"Yeah, we'll be sure to do that." Blake nodded vigorously. "Every chance we get, in fact."

Wynn punched him on the shoulder and started back to her post. "How did you ever end up with someone nice like Martha?"

Blake let the remark pass as he grabbed Martha to finish the dance. By the time five more numbers were over, Martha was begging for a respite, so Blake led her back to their table and they sat down.

"God, this thing is hot — " He pulled his mask out a little ways from his face, fanning himself.

"Take it off for a while, why don't you?"

"What! And blow my disguise! What I'm really wondering about is eating with this thing on. You hungry?"

"Starved."

Blake nodded, fixing the death face into place. "Rest that arm. I'll be back in a second."

Martha waved and leaned back in her chair, allowing herself a long, luxurious stretch. It suddenly came to her that she was really enjoying herself — that she wasn't worrying — and she couldn't even remember a night anymore when she hadn't been afraid. Maybe this whole thing had been blown out of proportion after all — and it really was just a prank, someone playing a sick joke — and Dennis really *had* died a year ago — and the calls, the awful fears, all just unfortunate coincidences. She believed that could happen — that it *did* happen — and maybe it was time to start accepting that she'd just been an innocent victim — *Story of my life, Martha Stevenson in the wrong place at the wrong time.* . . .

Having come to some kind of resolution at last, Martha smiled and stretched again, letting her eyes wander lazily over the dancing shadows on the floor . . . the fiendish orange grins throwing bizarre shapes up the walls. . . .

"Martha — "

"Oh, Wynn, you scared me again! You've got to stop sneaking up on me like that — "

"Martha — oh God, Martha — he's *back* — "

The hands on her arm were clamped so tightly

that Martha winced. She struggled to turn in her chair, and the green witch face was twisted in fear, the mascara-ringed eyes nearly bulging from Wynn's head.

"What?" Martha repeated dumbly. "What did you — ?"

"Dennis!" Wynn whimpered. "I saw him, Martha — *I saw Dennis*!"

The blood froze in Martha's veins. She looked down stupidly at Wynn's fingers cutting into her arm . . . up at Wynn's horrified features. "Oh . . . my God . . . are you *sure*? Are you — ?"

"In the crowd!" Wynn's voice sank to a terrified whisper. "I looked up and he was standing there — *just standing there — watching* me!"

Martha's mind wouldn't work. She pulled on Wynn's hands, her words jumbled and slow. "Are you positive? How could it be, it can't be, it — "

"I don't know how long he'd been standing there, but when he realized I'd seen him, he just disappeared — he — " She gave Martha a shake. "Martha — he could be *anywhere*! Why is he *here*, Martha? He's *dead*! *Why is he here?*"

"Wynn — calm down — let's find Blake — "

"Oh, God, what am I going to do!" Wynn turned from side to side, all reason surrendered to panic, and Martha grabbed her by the shoulders.

"Wynn, we've got to find Blake and Greg — just calm down — "

"Where *are* they? Hurry, Martha — "

"Blake went to get us some food. Didn't you see him?"

184

Wynn shook her head mindlessly. "No — I didn't see anyone — just . . . Dennis — "

"Come on." Steering Wynn firmly in front of her, Martha threaded her way through the grotesque throng, craning her head, trying to spot Blake. Finding anyone was hopeless in this mess, she realized with a sinking feeling, and already Wynn was cold to the touch. How much more, Martha wondered — *how much more of this can she take?* She thought of yelling, but the music was so loud, she could barely hear herself think. *It could be anyone.* . . . Wynn stumbled and Martha righted her again before they both fell. Where was Blake — and Greg? In the awful, throbbing darkness all the ghoulish faces looked alike — evil and deadly — *It can't be Dennis . . . it's impossible . . . oh God, he's not dead!*

"I'm going to be sick," Wynn mumbled, and Martha barely caught the words before she felt the heaving of Wynn's body.

"Go on into the bathroom." Martha gave her a push. "You'll be safe there. I'll try to find Blake and Greg."

"Come with me!"

"No, Wynn, we've got to find the boys — we've got to get some help!"

Wynn nodded, her hand clamped over her mouth, and Martha watched her staggering drunkenly through the mob, disappearing at last down the hall that led to the restrooms.

She felt like she was trapped in a snake pit. An insane asylum. The worst kind of nightmare. On every side of her demonic faces laughed and leered, pinning her in, blocking her escape.

"Blake!" She cupped her hands around her mouth, and shouted, feeling foolish, knowing it was useless. The faces still laughed, mocking her. She shoved her way through them, elbowing people aside. *If Dennis is here, then he's after me . . . I'm the one he wants. . . . I'm the one he wanted all along. . . .*

From the farthest corner of her brain she heard her name being called — but still — still — it didn't register at first. And when it finally sank in, there was only the briefest flash of hope that it was Blake, until slowly she realized that it was the lead singer of the band — the singer interrupting the song — nodding at a masked figure near the stage and saying again into the microphone: "Martha Stevenson. Martha Stevenson? Hey, Martha, you've got a phone call in the locker rooms — Martha Stevenson?"

A general chorus of catcalls and whistles followed her as she ran — and then she was stumbling into the back room and grabbing the receiver from a bored chaperone who used that opportunity to escape for refreshments.

"Hello?" she gasped. "Hello, this is Martha — "
And he laughed.

He laughed and he laughed, even though the effort left him breathless, and the laugh was quiet and horrible and smug while Martha screamed into the phone —

"You leave me alone! Whoever you are, do you hear me? You — "

"There's no one home, Elizabeth," he said. "It's Halloween . . . and they're all dead."

My God . . . my God, no! "What have you done to Conor! *What have you done to him!*"

"Trick or treat, Elizabeth," the voice whispered.

It wasn't laughing anymore.

Chapter 17

It was like one of those horrible dreams where you ran and got nowhere, and screamed but nobody heard. . . .

Martha didn't even remember getting from the locker room back to the gym — suddenly she was at the door and running outside, and she wondered desperately how she'd managed to fight her way through the crowds. Rain was coming down in sheets, and as she stood there crying helplessly, someone called her name and grabbed her from behind.

"Martha — " It was Blake's voice behind the mask, the face of Death, and Martha pulled away with a cry. "Hey, whoa, what is it? Didn't you hear me calling you back there? What's — "

"I've got to go home!" Martha sobbed. "Something's happened to Conor!"

"What?" Blake spun around as Wynn ran out behind him. "Here she is, Wynn — I found her — "

"Martha, what's the — ?" Wynn stopped in her

tracks as if some sense warned her of what she didn't want to hear.

"You were right, Wynn!" Martha's voice rose, practically hysterical. "I just got a phone call — and he said Conor was *dead!*"

"Right about what?" Blake sounded totally baffled. "Would you two mind telling me what's going on?"

"You won't believe me!" Wynn cried.

"Wynn," Blake's face went serious, "come on now — "

"I saw Dennis!"

"He didn't die like everyone thought — he's the one who's been threatening me — he thinks I'm Elizabeth — " Martha joined in.

Blake's head was spinning between them; he took a step back as if he'd been struck.

"What . . . what are you saying?"

"I can't explain now!" Martha nearly screamed at him. "Take me *home,* Blake — *please!*"

"Wynn, where's Greg?" Blake demanded, but even as Wynn shook her head, he was running back into the gym.

Wynn put her arms around Martha, and they clung to each other.

"Oh, Wynn — if Conor's hurt, I'll never forgive myself — "

Wynn had never sounded so terrified. *"What's happening?"*

Hell, Martha wanted to say, *hell is what's happening,* but at that moment Blake and Greg burst out onto the walkway and herded them to Blake's car. In another minute they were racing on the blacktop out of town.

"Damn it, watch the road!" Greg snapped as they skidded around a curve. "It's slick as hell out here. Now, will someone please tell me what's going — "

"Okay, okay, I've got it under control." Blake swerved the car, throwing them all to one side, then wiped angrily at the foggy windshield. "Use a rag on this, will you? I can't see where I'm going."

Muttering to himself, Greg searched through the glove box, then wiped a handful of tissues across the glass, leaving strips of soggy paper. Martha, clenching Wynn's hand for dear life, had a sudden crazy urge to laugh — in all the excitement they'd forgotten to take off their masks — *a gypsy, a witch, and an executioner all bound for fate in a car driven by Death. . . .*

A squeal of tires jolted her back to the present — as lightning crackled dangerously close, Blake saw the fallen tree limb just in time to jerk the car and miss it. Greg cursed under his breath and wedged himself back against the door.

"You're going to kill us all, you know that?"

It could be anyone . . . anyone. . . .

"Oh, Conor," Martha whispered, "please don't be dead. . . ." And as they reached the house at last, she saw the light in Conor's window.

"Martha — wait!"

Martha heard Blake's shout as she jumped from the still-moving car — Ripping off her mask, she felt the slosh of mud and water as she ran heedlessly up the drive and burst through the front door —

"Conor!" she screamed. "Conor!"

And the silence was lifetimes long, as she stumbled up the stairs, fell out onto the landing —

"Conor!"

"Martha?" His voice came back—hoarse and weak — but *alive* — and footsteps came rushing into the lower hall and she heard Conor pulling on his clothes. "What are you doing home? What's going on?"

She was halfway through his door when the lights went out.

She heard voices, muffled and surprised, bodies falling over one another in the dark —

She heard Conor searching for the light switch.

She heard the soft sliding sound in the wall.

For one agonizing instant she couldn't place it, couldn't quite recognize what it was — what it meant —

Until she finally moved into Conor's room —

And knew that they weren't alone.

It was then that the icy pinpricks started up her arms, turning her spine to jelly, raising the hair at the back of her neck —

"Conor?" she whispered.

Something moved deep in the shadows. Something that wasn't Conor. Something that seemed to have stepped out of the wall and now waited to see what they would do.

As Martha stood there, blind and helpless, the bodies recovered themselves from the first floor and began to stumble up the stairs. And one of them shouted her name —

In that instant the shadows gathered and sprang. Martha heard a groan, and there was a soft hiss of metal slashing darkness — as something fell beside her, Conor's hand came out of nowhere and closed around her own —

"Come on, Martha — *hurry!*"

She let him pull her like a rag doll. She heard his hand frantically groping along the wall.

Wet fingers slid over her ankle.

Shrieking, she pitched forward into sudden nothingness, crumpling down into a tiny space of darkness. She sensed that they were in a passageway of some kind, but she couldn't figure out how they'd gotten there. Martha could feel Conor's body pressed against her, hear his hoarse struggle to breathe — and then she could hear the wall — *the wall!* — sliding shut and hands beating on the other side, and Conor's urgent whisper, "We've got to run, Martha — we're trapped behind the wall — "

The space was so tight they could barely fit side by side. Somehow Conor squeezed ahead of her, and as she heard him slip and throw out his arms, she realized they were on a narrow stairwell. Conor's fingers found hers, closed and tightened, pulled her down . . . down. . . . Terrified, Martha slid her way behind him, gasping as spiderwebs clung to her face.

Without warning Conor stopped, and Martha crashed into him with her cast. She could hear his hands scrabbling against wood.

"Where are we, Conor? Where are we?"

"I don't know — " The answer came out in a

gasp, and Martha was suddenly aware of his shirt, soaked and stuck to his side. At first she thought it was his fever, but as she rubbed her fingers together, the wetness was too thick for sweat.

"Oh God, Conor, you're bleeding — "

"Am I?" he said weakly.

She could feel him now, shivering uncontrollably. She slipped off her shawl and knotted it around him. Sliding her arms about his waist, she pressed her head against his back and prayed.

Without warning the wall opened up, and they fell through.

For several seconds Martha was too stunned to move. She lay there in a tangled heap with Conor, her heart hammering against stone, and she realized they were on the floor. It was damp and freezing cold, and as she opened her eyes, there was only blackness.

"I . . . think . . . we're somewhere in the cellar," Conor gasped. He was seized by another fit of coughing, and Martha tried to pull him into a sitting position.

"But *where* in the cellar? Oh, Conor, you're really hurt — what are we gonna do?"

"Listen." His hand came down on her arm, trying to steady himself.

"What? I don't hear anything."

"That's what I mean. We're not being followed anymore."

Martha's heart skipped a beat. "Then . . . where is he? Where are *we*?" Her whisper echoed ghostly in the icy air. From somewhere in the distance came a steady drip of water, and dampness lay thick around them, heavy and stale.

"Wait! Oh, Conor, wait a minute!" With a flash of hope, Martha fumbled in her pocket and pulled out the packet of matches Greg had given her. "I think there's a few left. Conor, Wynn said she saw Dennis at the party! You were right — he never died in that accident — he's been waiting all this time — "

Conor was having trouble getting the matches open. He was gasping so hard for air that Martha reached out in alarm.

"Let me — I can light them." She struck one and Conor took it between trembling fingers, moving it through the air in a flickering arc.

They seemed to be in some sort of storage closet. Most of three walls were covered with rotted shelving, old bottles, jars, and crumbling boxes; the fourth wall was taken up by a huge door. Conor let the match drop and Martha quickly lit another, taking in the mildew, broken glass, seeping puddles across the stone floor. . . .

"Help me with the door," Conor said breathlessly.

"No, don't do it, Conor, let me. You keep lighting matches."

"Save the matches — we may need them — "

In the darkness once more, Martha heard Conor trying the handle, but it wouldn't open. Together they braced their shoulders against it and shoved, but the door wouldn't budge.

"I'll scream for help," Martha said. "Greg and

Blake and Wynn are in the house somewhere — they'll be looking for us — they'll hear us and — "

The laugh came without warning . . . filling the cellar . . . echoing from each black corner . . . rising . . . then fading on the other side of the locked door.

Martha's blood chilled within her. Frozen where she stood, she heard the slow, deliberate footsteps . . . the slow, demonic chuckle from the unseen face. . . .

"No one will ever hear you again," the voice said. "No one will hear you . . . and no one will find you."

Martha's mind went into a frenzy. *That voice — that voice on the phone —*

"I'm the one who really loved you . . . don't you see? I would have loved you best of all. . . . But no — you always wanted to be together." The voice sounded sad. "And now you will be. Forever."

In the dark the next sound was deadly.

In the dark it was an explosion, but in some part of Martha's mind it was only a small spurt of flame. . . .

"Trick or treat," the voice said.

And in the hissing, crackling quiet, a tendril of smoke curled beneath the door . . . curled into Martha's face.

"It's a fire," Martha said, and she reached for Conor in the dark. "He's going to burn us alive."

Chapter 18

The blackness surged in, thick and suffocating, and the blackness was her mind, her world, all her hope, and she was falling, falling, and something was trying to pull her back —

"Martha, come on," Conor choked, his hands like icicles through her clothes "you can't give up now — there has to be a way out of here — "

"He thinks I'm Elizabeth," she said numbly, "and he thinks you're Blake, and all this time he's been plotting — waiting for just the right time — and we fell right into his hands — "

"Martha, snap out of it!" Conor's hand slapped at her cheek, but there was no strength in it, and he was so cold . . . so cold. . . . She heard him crawling back to the secret passageway . . . scraping at the wall . . . fighting for breath. . . . "It won't open . . . we can't get out this way. . . ."

"Here." Martha felt like a robot, her body moving through no will of her own. "You light the matches and I'll look. You need to save your strength."

"I'm . . . okay. . . ." He bent double in another

siege of coughing, and Martha knew it was more than just the cold now. In the glow of the match she could see dark red drops around his feet, the long dark stream down the side of his jeans, the rip through his shirt. And now the shadows were thickening with pale, gray smoke. She could see a glow under the door, and as Conor lit another match, she began to pound for all she was worth.

"Help!" she screamed. "*Somebody!* Let us out of here! Oh, Conor — why aren't they coming? He must have done something to them — " She looked down in dismay, felt the raw sting of her hands, heard the flames licking at the door. Her throat was already beginning to burn.

"Get down on the floor," Conor said softly. "It's . . . easier to breathe."

We're going to die. The realization came calmly and quietly, and she looked at Conor's face in the dying glow of the match flame. *We're going to die and he knows it and he doesn't want me to be afraid.* . . .

"I'm sorry, Conor," she whispered.

"Sorry? For what?"

"For everything . . . for causing you so much trouble . . . for getting you into this."

He tried to laugh, but it ended in a moan. "You sound . . . like you don't think we'll get out of here."

"I don't think we will. You don't, either, do you?"

"You never did . . . know me very well. . . ."

She felt his hand on her head . . . the brief touch of his cheek against her hair. . . .

Blinking back tears she threw her arms around

him and was shocked at how frail he suddenly felt.

"The shelves, Martha," he whispered, "something to break down the door — "

And she did it, not because she believed it would work, but because he was so determined and she wanted *him* to believe. She crawled to one wall of shelves and began ripping the sagging boards, and suddenly — suddenly — she jumped up with a shriek.

"Are you all right?" There was real fear in Conor's voice this time, and Martha stared at him, too shocked for a moment to answer.

"Conor, there's something *behind* here!" she gasped. "I think it's a . . . a *tunnel* or something — "

Conor struck the last match, straining to peer through the smoky darkness.

"It isn't even boarded up — it's just got junk piled in front of it like someone wanted to hide it!"

The match sputtered . . . went out.

"Let's go," Conor said.

It was scarcely more than a crawl space. As Conor pulled himself along on his uninjured side, Martha struggled with her cast and crept behind him in a daze of terror. The tunnel echoed with Conor's labored breathing and the soft scurrying of rats — and she had the most horrible feeling that they were crawling deeper and deeper into the earth, farther and farther from help, the darkness going on and on forever.

When Conor suddenly stopped moving, Martha

threw herself on him in a panic. "Conor! Are you — ?"

"A door . . . there's . . . a door at the end," Conor said, and Martha heard his fists scraping wood, each sound weaker and weaker. . . .

"Conor!" She shook him violently, a shiver of danger rippling through her from head to toe. "It's opening — "

The groan of old, old hinges echoed through the dark.

And as the opening widened, it filled the tunnel slowly with hazy light.

Martha felt Conor's hand tighten on her own . . . pull her forward as he staggered to his feet into the light. . . .

"Martha . . ." he whispered, and she felt him stumble, felt his ice-cold hands go even colder — "we're in the mausoleum."

For one split instant her mind went totally blank — and *no, this isn't real, I'm only in a dream, I'll wake myself up, I'll make myself wake up now — right now —* and she floated ahead, still in a dream, *still led by Conor through a harmless, wondrous dream.* . . .

The light hurt her eyes.

Hazy and bright all at once, pulsing through the shadows . . . clawing up the walls where the dead lay in their quiet places . . . dancing in the fiery ring around an altar wreathed with candles. . . .

An altar wreathed with candles. . . .

And the stale, faded sweetness of dead flowers. . . .

Of death. . . .

And she felt Conor's arm go around her, turning her away, away from the lights, away from the hundreds of flickering candle flames —

"Don't look, Martha — "

"Conor, what *is* it? What's there?"

"No," Conor said, and he sounded so strange — and *no, I don't want to hear this, I won't listen, it's not real —*

"Martha," Conor said, "I think we just found Dennis."

And Martha, staring back at him in horrified disbelief, saw something else suddenly gliding up behind him, the tall black figure floating from the shadows, its Death face reflecting the hundreds of tiny, tiny lights —

"Conor, watch out!" she screamed.

The knife flashed down . . . slicing the darkness . . . ripping into Conor's shoulder. . . .

She saw him jerk forward . . . slide to the ground at her feet. . . .

And Death bending over him, the knife oozing blood onto the floor. . . .

"Dennis," the voice scolded, "how did you get out?"

And then Death looked straight into Martha's eyes.

"Elizabeth . . . why are you making me do this again?"

Martha staggered backwards, eyes fixed in terror as Death stood there quietly, watching. Beneath Conor a dark pool was widening over the floor.

"Why?!" Martha screamed. "Why are you *doing* this?" Her hands were out, reaching for Conor, but Death stepped between them. "Can't you see? I'm *not* Elizabeth! I'm *Martha*! Elizabeth's *dead*! You *killed* her!" And Martha was crying now, moving back as Death came closer. "Why did you do it, Blake?" she sobbed. "You couldn't have hated Dennis that much — you couldn't have been that afraid of losing Elizabeth — you could have had anything you wanted — "

Vey slowly the black sleeve raised. The twelve-inch blade glittered and sparkled in the light.

"I want *you*, Elizabeth," he hissed. *"Trick or treat!"*

Martha never had time to scream.

She saw the blade plunging down —

And the tiny flames scattering like sparks as doors burst wide and wind and rain roared through the tomb and two bodies hurled themselves forward, flinging Death away —

And then she heard the screaming —

The wild, insane screaming as Death thrashed and twisted in Blake's arms —

"Blake . . ." Martha murmured.

"Greg, call an ambulance!" Blake shouted, and he was wrestling the mask away, tearing the knife from clenched hands, throwing the heaving body to the floor as the long brown hair spilled out around the contorted face — "They're dead — do you hear me, Wynn? Both of them . . . dead."

Chapter 19

"Conor!" Martha knelt beside his prone figure, touched his side, his shoulder, drew back a bloody hand. "Oh, Blake, I think he's — "

"He's not dead. Here — hold this against him. Hold it tight." Keeping one eye on Wynn, Blake stripped out of his black cape and lay it over Conor, then took off his shirt and pressed it to Conor's shoulder. Conor's face was ashen, but his eyes fluttered open, trying to focus on the two faces bending over him.

"Hey, you're gonna be okay — you hear that?" Blake squeezed Conor's hand. "Just hang on, man — hang on."

Conor's eyes clouded, pain and confusion glazing them over. His head moved, searching for Martha. "You . . . okay?"

His lips barely moved, and Martha leaned close to him, forcing a reassuring smile.

"Thanks to you . . . be quiet now, the ambulance is on its way — " Her eyes widened in alarm as his hand slid from her arm. "Blake!"

Blake searched for a pulse and nodded grimly. "He just passed out. Keep that against him."

"Why didn't you let me keep him, Elizabeth?" the voice from the corner said. It wasn't Wynn's voice, but it was coming from Wynn's mouth, and a stranger stared out at them from Wynn's dull eyes. She drew her knees up, curling herself into a ball, and began to rock, very slowly, watching them.

"You thought you loved Dennis, didn't you, Wynn?" Blake said softly. "Why didn't you tell us how you felt?"

The eyes grew dark with a dangerous hate. Martha pressed against Conor, as if she could shield him from it.

"You hated him," Wynn said. "You would have fixed it so we couldn't be together."

"He didn't love you, Wynn," Blake said. "He loved Elizabeth."

"Elizabeth . . . Elizabeth . . . Elizabeth . . ." she chanted softly. "Elizabeth didn't want him. Elizabeth was through with him. I couldn't let him go back to her . . . he'd never have known how much *I* loved him. I was the one, you know. . . ." The eyes were coldly smug. "I was the one who loved him best."

Blake looked down at the floor. On the other side of the room a few candles still flickered around the makeshift altar, throwing grisly shadows over the stone walls and faded markers . . . shadows of something that might once have been human. . . .

"You followed them that night, didn't you?" Blake said quietly.

"I followed them. I *had* to follow them. The calls didn't work, and the threats didn't work, and they were going to *talk* that night, he was going to *convince* her to come back to him. . . ." The eyes closed, only for an instant, then popped open, glittering. "I had him all to myself for a while . . . I had someone who loved me — "

"He didn't love you. He was using you."

"Don't you *say* that! Don't you *ever say that!*"

Martha cowered back from the hate-filled eyes, but Blake met them straight on.

"He was using you to keep tabs on Elizabeth — "

"He *loved* me!" Wynn cried. "He wanted to stay with me!"

"So what did you do that night, Wynn? After you followed them home, how did you manage to get Elizabeth alone in her room?"

Wynn pondered a moment, a frown at the corners of her mouth. "I just went in. I just walked in, that's all. They didn't even hear me." Her features twisted at the memory. "They were in her room, and they were laughing . . . and I could hear them talking . . . and I could hear the bed . . . and they didn't even know I was there — "

Martha was staring down at Conor, at his bleached cheeks and bloodstained hair, at Blake's shirt going soggy in her shaking hands. She fought off a wave of nausea and shut her eyes.

"They thought I was a prowler," Wynn smiled. "I *made* them think that. I made just enough noise downstairs and I went to the cellar. And then Dennis came down, just like I knew he would. . . ."

Martha wanted to cover her ears, but she couldn't. The cast on her arm felt like dead weight. . . . The fingers on her other hand had gone numb from trying to staunch Conor's blood. . . .

"You hit him," Blake said softly. "Didn't you?"

Wynn nodded, her expression gone blank. "I had to. I had to do that." She traced a circle on the floor with her finger. "I took a knife from the kitchen. I went up the secret stairs to her closet. She was still on the bed waiting for him. She was smiling." Wynn shrugged, almost indifferently. "I didn't have a choice, really. I had to."

Blake turned away then, his face grave. He put up one hand as if to hold back the horrible images, but Wynn went on.

"She didn't really fight me," Wynn said, as if that still amazed her. "She was just so *surprised*. . . . It was really just so easy. . . ."

"What . . . did you do with Dennis?" Blake mumbled.

"I went back down to tell him the news — that we were finally *free* — but — but" — the eyes widened, the face crumpling in slow motion — "he wouldn't *answer* me, he wasn't *moving*, he wouldn't *talk* — " She took a deep breath, her voice going hard. "It was *Elizabeth's* fault — it was *her* fault Dennis got hurt — if she'd stayed away from him, he never would have . . . have. . . ."

Martha's heart clutched as Wynn began to uncoil and stand up. Blake positioned himself casually between them, but Martha could see his every muscle tensed. From the wildly flickering darkness near the front of the tomb came the cautious approach of footsteps.

"Greg?" Wynn called softly. "Greg, is that you?"

"Yes, Wynn, it's me."

And as Greg walked slowly towards them, Martha noticed for the first time how the tall, wide doors of the mausoleum were open, fresh cold air flooding the dank shadows.

"I was just telling them about Dennis," Wynn said anxiously. "I was going to tell them how I put his car there on the bridge — I was just — "

"Yes, sweetheart, I heard you."

Martha had never seen Greg so shaken, his face so white, his hands so unsteady. Gently, lovingly, he eased Wynn back to her sitting position on the floor and cast Blake a tragic look.

"The dream, Greg" — Wynn looked up into his face, and her voice was like a child's — "the dream I keep having, Greg. Have I told you about it? About the long . . . long . . . dark. . . ."

"Yes," Greg said sadly. "You told me about the dream."

The crawl space! Martha's head came up, and she locked stares with Blake, the meaning finally clear.

"The mausoleum," Martha murmured. "She brought Dennis here to the mausoleum — "

"It was Greg who figured it out," Blake said quietly. "When we couldn't find you or Conor and we smelled the smoke in the basement — " He paused, drew a deep breath. "After we put the fire out and broke down the door, that's when we saw the tun-

206

nel — Greg knew it had to lead away from the house. And then he remembered the stories about tunnels connecting with the cemetery — "

Martha reached up and clutched Greg's arm. His smile was wan. "Lucky I had my trusty axe, huh?" He stopped beside them, his hands clenching. "The police are on their way — I — " He shook his head and knelt beside Conor, shrugging out of his own costume now, tucking it around Conor's ribs.

Conor stirred slightly . . . and went quiet again.

"Greg," Wynn said plaintively, "are they going to take me away?"

Greg and Blake exchanged glances. "Yes," Greg said quietly, "someplace where you'll be safe."

Wynn looked from one to the other. "I don't think I can go. Dennis wouldn't want me to leave him, you see — that's why he wanted to come here — so he could be with *me*, and not Elizabeth — "

Martha saw the struggle on Greg's face as he tried to hide his revulsion . . . as he tried to avoid looking at the candles ringed around the thing upon the altar . . . as Wynn reached out her hand to him. . . .

"You won't let them take me, will you Greg? You won't, will you?"

Greg stepped away from the outstretched hand.

And Wynn sprang so suddenly that no one even saw her go for the knife.

With a shriek she threw herself on Martha, slamming her to the ground.

Martha felt the crack of stone against her skull. . . .

The shock of cold metal against her throat. . . .

Faraway voices blurred — shadows swarmed with lights and shouts and movements —

"Martha! Martha, can you hear me?"

And suddenly she was in Blake's arms, and over his shoulder she could see Wynn struggling, Wynn being dragged by three policemen — Wynn's face a demon's face, glaring at Martha in poisonous fury.

"Why'd you come back, Elizabeth?" she was shrieking, throwing herself from side to side. *"He's mine!* You can't have him! You should have listened to the warnings! You should be *dead* by now! You can't get away from me — I've been in the house all along — listening — *watching* — I killed you, Elizabeth — *you can't take Dennis away from me!"*

The mad shrieks faded into the night. Martha pulled herself from Blake's arms as Conor was lifted onto a stretcher.

"Be careful with him!" she pleaded. "Where are you taking him?" There were so many people in there now, so much confusion — glaring lights . . . flashbulbs popping . . . voices barking orders . . . a man with a notebook —

"Just take it easy, Miss. Is he a friend of yours?" The man nodded towards the stretcher being carried away. "Name?"

"My brother," Martha said. "Conor Wheelwright. My brother." She saw Greg deep in conversation with more policemen, felt Blake's arms around her again.

"He's going to be okay," he said. "They told me so. I promise."

"Oh, Blake — " As the horrors crumbled around her, she sagged against his chest, felt his kiss on her forehead. Tears rolled down her face and she shook her head. "Conor knew."

"Knew what?"

"The first time he and I found the cemetery, he had a bad feeling about the mausoleum," Martha remembered. "He felt some kind of danger." She squeezed her eyes shut, held back a sob. "Can we go to the hospital now?"

"Sure we can." His arms tightened around her. She felt his heart beating against her chest. "I almost lost you tonight," he said hoarsely. And he kissed her again — long and sweet — and when she finally opened her eyes, he was smiling. "Does Conor know how lucky he is?"

And Martha thought of Conor, so still and pale as he was taken away — how annoyed he'd be when he woke up to find himself in the hospital. And she saw herself beside his bed and Blake there with her, and how that look would creep across Conor's face, and how she wouldn't even mind —

She looked into Blake's warm brown eyes and kissed him tenderly, right on his smile.

"I'm the lucky one," Martha said.

And she meant it.

About the Author

RICHIE TANKERSLEY CUSICK was born and raised in New Orleans, Louisiana. She now lives with her husband, Rick, a designer and calligrapher, and their cocker spaniel Hannah, just outside Kansas City, Missouri.

Ms. Cusick is also the author of the Scholastic Point paperback *The Lifeguard*. She likes to keep her studio dark while writing, and often listens to the movie soundtracks from *Psycho* and *Nightmare on Elm Street* when she's looking for a particular mood.

Halloween is, of course, one of her favorite holidays.

GREEN WATCH by Anthony Masters

GREEN WATCH is a new series of fast moving environmental thrillers, in which a group of young people battle against the odds to save the natural world from ruthless exploitation. All titles are printed on recycled paper.

BATTLE FOR THE BADGERS

Tim's been sent to stay with his weird Uncle Seb and his two kids, Flower and Brian, who run Green Watch – an environmental pressure group. At first Tim thinks they're a bunch of cranks – but soon he finds himself battling to save badgers from extermination . . .

SAD SONG OF THE WHALE

Tim leaps at the chance to join Green Watch on an anti-whaling expedition. But soon, he and the other members of Green Watch, find themselves shipwrecked and fighting for their lives . . .

DOLPHIN'S REVENGE

The members of Green Watch are convinced that Sam Jefferson is mistreating his dolphins – but how can they prove it? Not only that, but they must save Loner, a wild dolphin, from captivity . . .

MONSTERS ON THE BEACH

The Green Watch team is called to investigate a suspected radiation leak. Teddy McCormack claims to have seen mutated crabs and sea-plants, but there's no proof, and Green Watch don't know whether he's crazy or there's been a cover-up . . .

GORILLA MOUNTAIN

Tim, Brian and Flower fly to Africa to meet the Bests, who are protecting gorillas from poachers. But they are ambushed and Alison Best is kidnapped. It is up to them to rescue her *and* save the gorillas . . .

SPIRIT OF THE CONDOR

Green Watch has gone to California on a surfing holiday – but not for long! Someone is trying to kill the Californian Condor, the bird cherished by an Indian tribe – the Daiku – without which the tribe will die. Green Watch must struggle to save both the Condor and the Daiku . . .

MYSTERY THRILLERS

Introducing a new series of hard-hitting action-packed thrillers for young adults.

THE SONG OF THE DEAD by Anthony Masters
For the first time in years "the song of the dead" is heard around Whitstable. Is it really the cries of dead sailors? Or is it something more sinister? Barney Hampton is determined to get to the bottom of the mystery . . .

THE FERRYMAN'S SON by Ian Strachan
Rob is convinced that Drewe and Miles are up to no good. Where do they go on their night cruises? And why does Kimberley go with them? When Kimberley disappears Rob finds himself embroiled in a web of deadly intrigue . . .

TREASURE OF GREY MANOR by Terry Deary
When Jamie Williams and Trish Grey join forces for a school history project, they unearth much more than they bargain for! The diary of the long-dead Marie Grey hints at the existence of hidden treasure. But Jamie and Trish aren't the only ones interested in the treasure – and some people don't mind playing dirty . . .

THE FOGGIEST by Dave Belbin
As Rachel and Matt Gunn move into their new home, a strange fog descends over the country. Then Rachel and Matt's father disappears from his job at the weather station, and they discover the sinister truth behind the fog . . .

BLUE MURDER by Jay Kelso
One foggy night Mack McBride is walking along the pier when he hears a scream and a splash. Convinced that a murder has been committed he decides to investigate and finds himself in more trouble than he ever dreamed of . . .

DEAD MAN'S SECRET by Linda Allen
After Annabel's Uncle Nick is killed in a rock-climbing accident, she becomes caught up in a nerve-wracking chain of events. Helped by her friends Simon and Julie, she discovers Uncle Nick was involved in some very unscrupulous activities . . .

CROSSFIRE by Peter Beere
After running away from Southern Ireland Maggie finds herself roaming the streets of London destitute and alone. To make matters worse, her step-father is an important member of the IRA – if he doesn't find her before his enemies do, she might just find herself caught up in the crossfire . . .

THE THIRD DRAGON by Garry Kilworth
Following the massacre at Tiananmen Square Xu flees to Hong Kong, where he is befriended by John Tenniel, and his two friends Peter and Jenny. They hide him in a hillside cave, but soon find themselves swept up in a hazardous adventure that could have deadly results . . .

VANISHING POINT by Anthony Masters
In a strange dream, Danny sees his father's train vanishing into a tunnel, never to be seen again. When Danny's father really does disappear, Danny and his friend Laura are drawn into a criminal world, far more deadly than they could ever have imagined . . .